Brown Rabbit: her story

Brown Rabbit:
her story

Evangeline Morse
Illustrated by DAVID STONE MARTIN

FOLLETT PUBLISHING COMPANY

CHICAGO · NEW YORK

Library of Congress Catalog Card Number: AC 66-10625

First Printing

Follett Publishing Company
1010 West Washington Boulevard
Chicago, Illinois 60607

T/L 0864

For Corine

Brown Rabbit: her story

1

The taxi pulled away from the curb and sped south on Mount Vernon Street. Ceretha Jane Brown, her mother, father, and big sister Ruth stood on the sidewalk surrounded by luggage.

Ceretha, better known as Brown Rabbit, surveyed the tall, ugly, brick building with a tailor shop on the ground floor. Her mouth quivered a little as she turned toward her father, "Oh, Papa, I'd hoped it would be a little house with a yard all around it."

Papa opened his mouth, but no words came out. Instead, he snapped his mouth closed and reached for several of the bags.

Ruth Ann answered for Papa. "Houses to rent are very hard to find here, dear. Bert and I did our best. Maybe it will be only for a little while."

All this time Mama had said nothing. She grasped Ceretha Jane's hand and held it tightly. Ceretha looked up at her mother. Mama's soft brown eyes looked as they did when Ceretha came to her with a cut or scratch to be bandaged. As she dressed the wound, Mama would say, "Don't fret, Brown Rabbit. In almost no time at all, it will heal, and you will have forgotten it."

Ruth Ann was helping Papa with the luggage and pointing, "We go this way, Papa—to the right. We couldn't get a front apartment."

The four of them made their way around the side of the building. Several dirty children ran to the entrance and stared. A woman came to the door of the tailor shop and stared, too.

Ruth Ann kept talking to Papa as they walked to the rear of the place. Occasionally Papa would nod his head, nothing more. They came to a halt at a door underneath some wooden steps which led to the rear apartments above.

Suddenly, Papa asked, "Ruth Ann, when do I start at this job Bert's found for me?"

"You report Monday, Papa. We thought you'd want to rest a day or two."

"Great God from Zion, a man don't need rest in a place like this."

There were tears in Ruth's eyes as she fumbled in her purse for the key. Papa set the baggage down on the cement walk and put his hand on Ruth's shoulder. "I'm sorry. I know you've done your best. God helping us, 'twon't be long before things'll be the way they were back home. He turned and smiled at Ceretha Jane, who was still clinging to Mama's hand.

Ruth Ann found the key. As she was about to open the door, she said, "Mama, Bert and I arranged the furniture as best we could. Some of it had to be stored. I left the little personal things for you to do. You're to have supper upstairs with us tonight. We eat at six this week. Bert's working eight to four."

"Like always, Ruth Ann, you're being very thoughtful. Thank you. Come on, Brown Rabbit, it's the people that make the home." With those words, Mama was across the doorsill and into the kitchen.

Once she was inside the kitchen, Ceretha Jane began to take stock of things. Actually the kitchen was not too different from the one back home in New Hope, Mississippi. All the familiar pieces of furniture were here.

"Look, Mama," she exclaimed with delight, "Ruthie's hung our very best kitchen curtains. We used to save these for holidays. They're my favorites 'cause the red and white ruffles match the stool

11

Papa made for me. Where is my stool?"

"I thought you'd want it in your room," said Ruth. "Yours is the one off the living room. It's smaller than the one off the kitchen."

"I'll have to go and get it. It belongs right here at the table." Then Brown Rabbit patted the table a time or two. The things in this room were like long lost friends, a joy to see again. She touched each piece of furniture fondly. Mama, Papa, and Ruth stood watching every move she made. She stopped in front of the window which looked out into the backyard and alley beyond.

"Filthy, isn't it?" she proclaimed, rather than asked. "Come on, Ruthie, show us the rest of the house."

Ruth Ann reached for her little sister's outstretched hand and led the way across the kitchen to a bedroom.

"For you and Papa, Mama. There just wasn't room for your huge chest of drawers. It is among the things we stored, but I knew you could not part with your rocker, Papa. Close quarters, but it's here."

At this point, Brown Rabbit gave a leap and a squeal of delight and landed right in the middle of the old-fashioned four-poster bed, shoes and all. Ordinarily Mama would have scolded, but today she just smiled, as only Mama could smile. Papa beamed and said, in a preachery sounding voice, "Praise be, m' Rabbit's found her tongue and her legs."

"I'll be real careful of my feet, Mama," Ceretha said. "Your bed's one of the nicest places in the world. It's so soft and comfy." With a bounce, she was out of the bed as suddenly as she had pounced into it.

"Now, my room, Ruthie. Come on."

Back across the kitchen and through another door the four of them went.

"Don't stop here," Ceretha demanded as they entered the living room. "My room first." She rushed toward the first of two doors in the right wall.

"Not that one," cried Ruth. "That's the bathroom."

Ceretha was living up to her nickname. She had already bounded across the floor and was inside the other room. When the others reached her door, she was on her knees, hugging a long, wooden box. When she finally lifted her head, it was obvious that this was no ordinary box. It was made of white pine and had a beautiful rabbit carved on its lid.

"I was scared you'd put it away with the other things, Ruthie," she said, looking up from the chest. "Papa made it. I just couldn't bear to part with it."

"I know, Brown Rabbit. Papa used to make things for me, too."

Ceretha surveyed Ruth's face for a second or two. "Why'd you call me Brown Rabbit, Ruthie?

You never used to when you'd come home to visit."

"Well, I don't particularly like pet names nor nicknames, but sometimes they are a way of showing that you have very special feelings about someone. And you are strictly VIP to me. I guess that's why the Brown Rabbit came out."

"I don't mind the family calling me that, but I'd just as soon not have other people do it. You remember Miss Ronald? She taught you in the third grade, too. One time when you were at home she said that you got sophisticated after you graduated from junior college and came up North to live."

"Oh, she did?"

"I wasn't exactly sure what she meant, so I looked it up in the dictionary. There were so many definitions that I still wasn't sure, so I asked Miss Ronald what she meant. She said, 'Only that Ruth Ann's tastes have changed.' Is that good, Ruthie? Will I get sophisticated, too, now that I'm up North —maybe forever?"

"I doubt that Miss Ronald was paying me a compliment, really. I'm sure I have changed; I hope for the better. I don't think you need ever worry about becoming a sophisticate, but once this becomes home, you'll feel differently about a lot of things."

Ceretha rubbed her cheek against the rabbit on the chest. When she was certain that she could speak again without her voice quaking, she said, "Papa made all my furniture. He let me help him with some of the pieces. I rubbed the wood with fine steel wool and then fine sandpaper. Papa'd scold real bad if I didn't do a good job. 'Good wood deserves good workmanship,' he'd say. And then I'd have to go all over it again. We had such good times. On nice summer days, Mama'd bring her embroidery out into the backyard and sit near the shed and watch us. Maybe you can find some wood here to whittle on, Papa."

"Possibly, possibly," Papa mused.

"Work like Papa's is more than mere whittling, Brown Rabbit. Papa is a real woodcarver. That's just one of the many reasons I thought it best for you to come here to live. There are schools here where adults with talents like Papa's can develop them to the fullest," Ruth Ann added.

Papa turned on his heels and went back into the living room. "Don't you think it's about time we looked at our new parlor?"

When they followed, Papa was seated on the old leather-covered sofa bed and was in the process of lighting his pipe. This time it was Mama who gave the furniture affectionate pats. From the expression on her face, each piece brought back some very special memory.

Ruth Ann sat in a big chair opposite Papa and watched her mother and father. Papa was still quite handsome, though he was graying much too fast for his age. Papa's features were sharply chiseled. Traces of the Indian in his ancestry showed in his face. Mama, too, was graying. There were streaks of gray at her temples and in the center front of her dark brown hair. Mama was not a pretty woman, but there was something very calm and serene about her face. Ruth Ann wondered if she had really been right in insisting that her parents sell their home and start all over again here. "It's really for Ceretha," she said half aloud.

"What did you say, Ruth Ann?" Mama asked.

"I was really thinking out loud, Mama. It doesn't seem possible that Ceretha's almost ten years old. That makes me pretty ancient. I was well in my thirteenth year, and the apple of Papa's eye, when you came along and took over the throne, Ceretha."

Ceretha winked at Ruth, turned cartwheels, and plunked herself beside Papa on the sofa.

Papa puffed solemnly on his pipe for a second, then he put his arm around his youngest daughter and said, "Yep, I'll never forget that day. I was on my way home from town, and I met Aunt Irene trudging up the highway. 'Harve,' she said, 'Rosie's got a fine lil' baby gal home waiting fuh you. Funny lookin' lil' critter, but she's healthy.' And as bad as I hate to admit it, Baby, Aunt Irene was right. You were a funny looking little thing—black eyes, twinkling like a baby bunny's, no nose to talk about, and I declare your ears stuck up."

"Now, Harve," Mama intervened, "true, Ceretha wasn't as pretty a baby as Ruth Ann, but she was an unusually smart one."

"Granted, granted," Papa agreed, as he gave a big belly laugh. "Yes, sir," he went on, "that Rabbit's been my gal right from the beginning. I took one look at her and said to Mama, 'This baby's a brown rabbit, that's what she is.' "

Ruth Ann broke into his reminiscing with, "If you folks are to have supper with Bert and me, I'd better go prepare it. In order to get to my apartment,

17

you will have to come back around to the street. The entrance is to the left of the tailor shop, and we're three flights up."

Ceretha looked up at Papa. He was no longer smiling. Perhaps, for a little while, he, too, had forgotten the ugly, treeless street. Ruth Ann and Mama left the room. Papa put his pipe out, put it back in his mouth, removed it again, and finally laid it on the arm of the sofa. "When Ruth Ann says once this becomes home, Brown Rabbit, she's not talking about the building or this apartment. There are little houses with yards all around them, even in this town."

Mama called from the kitchen, "Harve, you and Brown Rabbit come help me unpack the bags. There's lots that can be done in four hours."

"You know, Brown Rabbit," Papa said, "with God and Mama on our side, we're bound to win."

"I'll get my stool and be right there. I'm glad I'm big enough to help."

Mama took the little red clock from one of the suitcases and set it by Papa's watch.

In practically no time at all, the clothes were unpacked and hung in the proper closets, and many other small articles were put away. Just as Papa lifted a box marked FRAGILE to the table, Mama announced, "Goodness, it's five o'clock and nobody is bathed or dressed. It's a good thing there's hot and cold running water. Brown Rabbit, you get bathed first."

Like most little girls, Ceretha liked to dress up. She teased until Mama agreed to let her wear her next to her very best summer dress. Papa helped to coax Mama.

"After all, Rosie," he said, "first impressions do count. We would not want to embarrass Ruth Ann by appearing shoddy."

Mama vowed that the two of them always ganged up against her. So, although she thought her Brown Rabbit looked just as nice in her ginghams, tonight it would be the pale, blue linen with ribbons and socks to match, and white slippers.

At five minutes of six, they were all dressed. Ceretha looked lovingly at her parents, as they stood side by side, smiling fondly at each other.

"Mama," she finally said, "you and Papa are just beautiful. Somehow everything nice reminds me of home—New Hope, I mean. Will we be here long, Papa? I don't like this place."

Papa ignored the question. "Rosa Lee," he said, "you've forgotten something. We've all forgotten something."

Mama rapidly recalled the events of the long day. As far as she could remember, she had not forgotten anything. "I'm sorry, Harvey, but everything seems in order to me."

19

"At home we never began, nor ended the day without thanks to God. Neither of us prayed this morning."

"I did, Papa, on the train, but I guess God didn't hear my prayer."

Mama was quick to answer, "No, dear, God heard your prayer. He just had a different answer."

Ceretha wasn't sure that she understood, but she felt it was best not to ask anymore questions. Besides, Papa often said that God was too big for man to understand.

2

Ceretha awakened abruptly with a shudder. She
sat erect in her bed and listened. There was no
mistake about it. She had not been dreaming. The
horrible sound came again. Only this time the
hissing was louder and longer than previously.
While she was collecting her wits and trying to
recall how she came to be in this strange room, the
hissing came again. Each time it seemed to be closer
and louder. At the next especially loud hiss, Ceretha
was out of bed and across the room calling loudly
for Mama.

Mama met her in the living room. It was such

a relief to find Mama there as always.

"What is it, Mama?" Ceretha blurted out, pointing toward her room.

"I'm sorry it frightened you, dear. There's an exhaust pipe for the steam presses in the tailor shop. It must be just a few feet from your window. Papa and I noticed it this morning, too. I guess we were too excited to even hear it yesterday."

"Oh!" Ceretha said, much relieved. "Where is Papa?"

"We need a screen door for the kitchen. You know your papa. He's gone to find a door or the materials to make one. Suppose you hurry and wash up and dress so that you can eat your breakfast. Papa may need help."

At home, in the summer, Mama and Ceretha always wore dresses of the same color in the morning, so Ceretha had chosen a yellow and white check because Mama was wearing yellow. When she had tied the last ribbon, Mama kissed Brown Rabbit in the middle of her forehead, held her off at arms' length, and said, "As pretty a rabbit as there is in any briar patch."

And she was, too. Her reddish brown face had been scrubbed until it shone. Mama had parted her hair in the middle and brushed and brushed until it shone. Two neat pigtails, that ended with yellow bows, curled up just above her shoulders. Ceretha's cheeks were plump, and she had a determined little mouth and chin. As Papa had said, her nose was nothing to talk about; it was just there in the middle of her face, about the size of a fair-sized button. Her eyes were what people usually noticed first. They were inky-black and quick as lightning. Then there were her ears. They were rather large, but not at all ugly. Ceretha vowed that when she grew up and could wear her hair up or down, as she pleased, she'd cover them up for good.

With her arm around Mama's waist, she started for the kitchen, where her first breakfast in her new home was waiting for her.

"The rosebud dishes, Mama!" Ceretha was puzzled by the sight of the extra special dishes. They came out only for Thanksgiving, Christmas, Ruth Ann's wedding breakfast, and other special occasions.

"Why, Mama?"

"Sit down at the table, and while I am getting your breakfast, I'll give you three guesses."

"You and Papa had fancy company and didn't wake me."

"You're cold."

"Wait now, don't rush me. Let's see—August 10th—that's not a holiday. It's not anybody's birthday, though mine's week after next. I hate to give up, but—"

As she poured milk into a glass, Mama said, "This is an occasion for a celebration for us, dear. It is not only a new day, but a beginning of a new life for the three of us." Mama's eyes were a little misty.

"I understand, Mama." Ceretha bowed her head to bless the table.

Papa came in before Ceretha finished eating. He had not been successful in finding a screen door, but he had located a lumberyard and a hardware store. He laid several small packages on the floor just inside the door and asked, "Well, how's m' Rabbit this mornin'?"

When she had answered him and kissed him hard upon the cheek, Papa winked at Mama and announced, " 'Pears like I'll have to look elsewhere for a carpenter's assistant, Rosie. That Brown Rabbit's too prettied up for words."

With a mouth half full of cereal, Ceretha sputtered, "Now, Papa, you know I'm never too dressed up to help you. Besides, I can change in a hurry. I know exactly where my jeans are."

"An apron will do, I think," Mama answered.

"Accepted, accepted! By the time you finish eating and help Mama with the dishes, I'll probably be needin' help. The stuff was lots higher than I thought, Rosie, I bought a rake, too. Can't stand the sight of that filthy backyard." Out the door he went, with his toolbox and materials.

The dishes didn't take long, and Mama found a blue denim apron which she tied securely over Ceretha's clean dress.

"There!" Mama said, as she opened the door for Ceretha Jane. "I think you'll do."

Ceretha made no attempt to go out of the door.

"Mama," she said looking up, "maybe Papa'll plant some grass out there; then I won't hate it so."

Instead of answering, Mama gave Ceretha a gentle shove and closed the door.

Papa had found something on which to brace his wood and was sawing away. "Sit on the steps there. I've swept them off. I'm not quite ready for you to help me."

Ceretha sat down gingerly on the bottom step which led to the two rear apartments above. She sat quietly watching, when a tall, skinny, dusky girl of about ten years raced around from the front of the building. She stopped short when she saw Ceretha. The two girls sized each other up. Suddenly the strange girl seemed ill at ease. She could hear her mother's last words as she left for work that morning, "Bernadette, fuh goodness sake comb your hair befo' you go out in the street." Bernadette self-consciously gave her skirt a downward pull. It wasn't her fault that the dress she was wearing was neither green nor gray. The laundry had faded and shrunk it.

" 'scuse me," she said, as she whisked past Ceretha and dashed up the steps.

Papa lifted his head from his work with a start. "Did you speak to that girl as she passed?"

25

Ceretha answered slowly. She knew from the scowl on Papa's face that he was displeased.

"No, Papa, I didn't."

"And why not?"

"I don't really know, Papa, except I thought that maybe she might be the girl Ruthie was talking about last night at supper."

Papa stopped sawing. "I thought I made myself clear last night. I dislike snobbery of any kind. All Ruth Ann knows about that family is that they are poor and ignorant."

"She didn't speak to me either, Papa." Ceretha
was trying to justify her behavior to herself more
than to Papa. Papa went right on as if he hadn't
heard her. There was no use trying to make Papa
talk when he didn't want to talk. His refusal to
talk made it all the harder for Ceretha to ease her
conscience. She went over in her mind what Ruthie
had said the night before. She had pointed out that
there were only a few decent houses and families
with children on their block and that there was only
one girl of Ceretha's age in their building, but she

27

wouldn't like to have Ceretha play with her, because this family was terribly ignorant and the girl was always dirty.

That was when Papa lost his temper and scolded Ruthie about being snooty and some other things that Ceretha hadn't understood. Mama and Bert began to clear the table and Mama changed the subject by asking Ruthie where to find the markets.

"I'll speak next time, Papa. I'm sorry. Please don't be angry with me."

"All right, all right. But remember this, Brown Rabbit, 'Never judge a book by its cover.' Do you understand?"

"Yes, Papa."

Papa smiled and all was right again in Ceretha's world. She left her seat on the steps and went over to where he had begun to lay out the frame for the door.

"That was good timing. I was just going to ask you to lend a hand. Can you hold these two pieces steady while I put these corrugated joiners in place?"

Ceretha and Papa made an excellent team. Many times she seemed to sense just the thing he needed next. It wasn't long before the new screen door was well on its way to completion. The outer frame and the crosspiece were finished when Ceretha became aware that they were being watched.

There, where the steps made their first turn, sat the girl with the gray-green dress. Her chin rested on her knees, and her lanky arms were wrapped around her legs. She had combed her hair as best she could and added a rumpled bow to her ponytail.

Ceretha smiled faintly and called, "Hi!"

"Hi!" The girl replied.

For a second or two nothing more was said, then Ceretha broke the silence. "Why don't you come down here and watch. Papa won't mind, will you, Papa?"

Papa, with his mouth full of nails, nodded affirmatively.

The girl, even though invited, came down the steps slowly. The children who looked like Ceretha had not been too kind to her in the year that she had lived here. Even when her feet had touched the pavement, she stood with one hand resting on the banister.

Again it was Ceretha who spoke. "I'm Ceretha Jane Brown, and this is my papa." She pointed proudly to her father, who, by this time, was kneeling on the ground tacking on the screening.

"Please t' meet cha. My name Bernadette Hughes. I lives upstairs, yonder."

"Bernadette," Ceretha repeated, "that's a pretty name. Mine's sort of old-fashioned. Papa's mother, my grandmother, was Ceretha, too. How old are you?"

"Ten, going on eleven. How old are you?"

"I'm nine, almost ten. My birthday's just two weeks off."

"You got brothers 'n sisters?"

"Just Ruthie. She's named for my other grandmother. She's grown and married. She lives in the front on the third floor. You've probably seen her."

"Oh, sho! She that pretty lady live right in front of us. She real high fallutin'."

Ceretha snickered and Papa looked up from nailing. From the expression on his face, Ceretha wasn't sure that it was exactly a compliment; so she quickly added, "You'd like Ruthie if you knew her. Have you any brothers or sisters?"

"Naw! Jes' me, and Mother Dear says that's a gracious plenty these days."

"Where's your Papa?"

"Upstairs. His shift change today. Then he go on midnights."

"Shifts?" Ceretha asked.

"Uh huh, you don't know what's shifts? Well, so many days they works days. Then they works fo' to twelve. Aftah that they works f'om midnight tell mornin'."

"Now I remember. Ruthie said something about Bert working eight to four this week. Bert's my brother-in-law, Ruthie's husband. You probably know him, too."

"I never see him much. Cain't you go out front an' play. Mo' room out there."

That did it. All morning Ceretha had been able to crowd that awful street out of her mind. She racked her brain for a good excuse. She'd have to go sooner or later, but just now she did not want to go "out front." When they had gone to Ruth Ann's last night, the sidewalk had been crowded with people standing around, leaning against the building, or sitting on the curb.

"Wo—wouldn't you just as soon see my treasures?" stammered Ceretha.

"What's them?"

"You'll like them." She reached for Bernadette's hand and asked Papa if he would mind working alone for a while.

"Not a-tall, Brown Rabbit, not a-tall," was his reply.

"What he call you?"

"Brown Rabbit. That's my nickname."

Bernadette came to a dead stop as Ceretha opened the kitchen door.

"You reckon yo' mother goin' to care ef I come in yo' house?"

"Mama's at home."

"That ain't what I talkin' about."

Mama came to the door between the living room and the kitchen.

"So you've found a playmate," Mama said, smiling at them. "That's good."

Mama's warm smile drove away all of Bernadette's fears, but the sight of Mrs. Brown's spotless apron and sunny yellow dress served to remind her

31

of her own faded dress. She stood there looking down at her feet.

"Mama," Ceretha began her introduction, "this is Bernadette Hughes. She lives on the same floor with Ruthie."

"I'm glad to meet you, Bernadette. I was afraid our Brown Rabbit was going to be pretty lonesome. It isn't always easy to meet people when you're a stranger in a city."

"Yes 'um," Bernadette replied. "I'm pleased to meet cha, I'm sure."

Because she was so ill at ease, she went on talking rapidly about her mother and herself. Telling the first things that came into her mind. Gradually, as she realized that Mrs. Brown was listening sympathetically, she slowed down. When she stopped for breath, Mrs. Brown suggested that the girls play in Ceretha's room.

"I want to show Bernadette my treasures and the things that Papa made," Ceretha said.

"That's a good idea. It looks as if it is beginning to shower a little, anyway. I hope Papa can finish that screen. It's dreadfully warm in here with that door closed. I'm going to see how Papa's coming along."

Bernadette was all eyes as they entered the living room. At the door of Ceretha's room, she stopped and put her hands on what would have been her hips had she not been so thin.

"Gracious, you lives mos' like a princess."

Ceretha studied her guest for a moment, then she said, "Bernadette, where are you from?"

"I come here las' April from a sugar plantation near Baton Rouge, Louisiana. Where yo' all from?"

"We're from Mississippi. I liked it there. I wish we could go back," Ceretha added sadly.

3

Saturday and Sunday went by like magic. Papa had finished and hung his door. He'd raked the rubbish from the yard into neat piles and put them in the alley, while the neighbors watched at a distance. Mama and Ceretha had done the marketing; only up here, Ruthie said, people called it shopping.

Papa was pleased to learn that there was a Presbyterian church close by. He had been an elder in the one at home. On Sunday, he and Mama and Ceretha had walked a block down the street to the eleven o'clock service. Ruth Ann had asked to take Ceretha to the Episcopal church to which she and

Bert belonged, but Mama had said, "You know how proud your Papa is of his Rabbit. He'll want her there beside him on this first Sunday."

Ceretha had worn her very best summer dress. It was white piqué and very pretty.

Now it was Monday. Mama and Ceretha were alone in the kitchen. Ceretha was watching Mama make a chocolate pudding.

"What will Papa do at the mill, Mama?" Ceretha asked.

"I don't rightfully know, dear."

"Will it be inside or out?"

"Inside, I'm sure."

"Papa won't like it then," Ceretha declared. "He's going to miss his gardens. President Bell said the college never had a better gardener."

"I know. We talked about it during those last days at home."

"I wish I understood things better, Mama. Bert says that Negroes here are fighting for equal rights, too."

"That's true, but there are differences. Here at least there are no cross burnings, night riders, or murders of Negro leaders. Your Papa's strong in mind and body, and he will eventually find the kind of work he wants. We won't be in this building forever, you know. Only last night Papa was saying that he was going to hold onto the money we got from the sale of the New Hope house until we could find exactly what we are looking for here."

Mama went to the stove with the pudding. Just then Bernadette tapped on the window and waved as she started up the steps.

"She must be coming from Mass. I hope she comes down right after breakfast," said Ceretha. "I told Ruthie I was playing with Bernadette, and she didn't like it, Mama, but she said that it was up to you and Papa. I tried to tell her that Bernadette is lots of fun, but Ruthie didn't really listen.

"Did you know that Bernadette's papa had to leave Louisiana just because he wanted to vote?" Without giving Mama time to answer, she went on, "I'll bet you, if Bernadette's mama didn't have to work, she'd keep her shining like a new penny."

Mama agreed and tested her pudding. It wasn't quite thick enough. Ceretha kept right on jabbering.

"Of course, Bernadette talks pretty badly, but she'll learn. I'll help her some every day. Remember how some of the children used to sound when they first came up to the lab school? Let me lick the pot, Mama."

Mama lifted the pudding off the stove, and Ceretha's stool went back to the table once more.

"Ceretha," Mama said, in the midst of her stirring, "have you met any of the other children in the neighborhood yet?"

Mama never called Brown Rabbit "Ceretha" except when she was very serious or peeved. When she did say "Ceretha," Ceretha sat up and took notice.

"No. I promised Bernadette I'd go for a walk with her today. I can't see that it will be any fun, though. Everything's so ugly around here."

"Ruth Ann says there are some pretty houses not too far from here. Maybe Bernadette knows where they are."

Mama handed Ceretha the pan and wooden spoon. She moved one finger around the edges of the pan and spoon; the pudding lasted longer that way.

"Papa'd be some disappointed in you, Brown Rabbit, if he thought you were a quitter. Are you going to let a few ugly old buildings and some people you don't even know frighten you so that you can't come out of hiding?"

"As Papa would say, 'Not hardly, Mama, not hardly.' "

Mama and Ceretha both felt better now that the bugbear was out in the open. Mama, who could always find some work to do, sat down to mend. Ceretha was getting the last of the pudding from the pan when Bernadette rapped on the screen door. She knocked even though she could be seen.

It didn't take an expert to tell that the girl had dressed with extra care. Her hair was short and unruly, but she had made a tight, little ponytail and tied a freshly washed and ironed piece of blue ribbon around it. The dress would not have been half bad if it had just had a little starch in it. It was white with a blue sailor collar. She wore well-worn saddle oxfords instead of the usual sneakers.

Mama said, "Why don't you come in, child? You're always welcome. Too bad you didn't get here earlier; you could have helped clean the pudding pot."

"There isn't a speck left now, Bernadette, so you're out of luck."

"Oh, that's all right. Mrs. Brown, kin Ceretha go walkin' with me? We'll watch good at the corners, an' we won't go far."

"If she can get the pudding off her face, she may go."

"That's easy done, Mama. I'll be ready in a jiffy, Bernadette."

In the bathroom, Ceretha looked herself squarely in the eye. It was easier to pretend that everything was the same while she was in the house where everything and everybody were familiar. When she faced Mama and Bernadette, there was no indication that she was not happy about the coming tour.

Mama straightened her belt and gave her a great, big hug, which Ceretha returned with equal force.

"Go along the two of you and be careful."

Just as they reached the door, Mama called to Bernadette, "Come back a minute, Bernadette. I've a kiss for you, too." The girls left hand in hand.

"Your Mama's jes' about the nicest lady I know, you know that?"

"I think so, too."

With Bernadette as an enthusiastic guide, Ceretha made her first tour. The drugstore on the corner of the block, just south of their house, was highly recommended by Bernadette.

"You know, Bernadette, I think I'm going to be glad I came with you. Let's stop for an ice cream cone."

"Mr. Ewin' gives the biggest cones for a dime. Ain't nobody else 'round heaps 'em like that. Look up the street a piece. On the other side is Wickham Playground. Look yonder, see them big gates?"

As they passed the playground, Bernadette explained that the large brick building beside it which looked like a school was Wickham House, a place where you could go to play and make things. During August, they had only outdoor programs. The playground was open, and there was day camping and baseball. At the next corner, they turned right so that Ceretha could see the Catholic church where Bernadette went. There were several nice "homey looking" houses in the next block, and when Ceretha inquired as to who lived in them, the reply was "mos'ly teachers an' people like that." It was a good five or six blocks to the elementary and high schools.

The lawns in front of the school buildings were

beautifully kept. Their spacious greenness gave Ceretha Jane a good feeling.

"I'll like going to school here. It sort of reminds me of the campus at home. All of the new buildings are red brick with white trimming."

Bernadette was anxious to show Ceretha the rest of the school grounds. She pointed out the gymnasium, the auditorium, the cafeteria, and then they made their way around to the wading pool and playground.

The swimming class at the high school had evidently just been dismissed. Girls carrying swimming caps and towels passed them. Some of them spoke to Bernadette, but none of them stopped to talk or offered to walk along with them. Just ahead of Ceretha and Bernadette, as they turned onto the main street, were three girls talking and having a good time.

"See them two on the outside? They lives in our block. 'Member that lil' house nearby the Babtist church? Got a high fence 'round it. That'n with the red hair live there. Her daddy, he teach at Wilson."

"I remember that house. It's a pretty one. Do you play with her?"

"Gracious me, naw. She too high and mighty. That other'n with the long plaits live by us, too. Her name Barbara Jean Smith. I like they house better'n Marlene's; that's the other girl's name.

Barbara house got a right fancy door with a big knocker on it. They got benetian blinds and a lil' bitty fence 'round the grass."

"Papa and Mama were talking about that house Sunday. Papa said it showed what could be done if people cared. Who's the third girl?"

"Celestine Rivers. Her daddy, he teach at Douglas High School an' her mama, she teach in kindygarden at Wilson."

"Do they live near us, too?"

"Indeedy, not!" Bernadette turned and pointed back. "Woodside, that's where she live. There's where there's some sho' nuf pretty houses. I'll take you over thata way sometime. Les go home by Main an' look in the store winders."

It was well past noon when Ceretha and Bernadette walked into the Browns' kitchen. The table was set for lunch. Mama had used one of her embroidered luncheon cloths and set places for three, with the green glass dishes Papa and Ceretha had given her one Christmas.

"Did you have a good time?" Mama asked. Then in the same breath she said, "Lunch is ready as soon as you've washed your hands."

Lemonade always tasted cooler when it was served in these tall, green glasses. Mama had peanut butter and jam sandwiches, and alongside each plate was a luscious golden peach. Ceretha could hardly wait until the blessing was said. Mama had to hear all about their walk, then they counted the days until school opened—there were exactly twenty-one.

Bernadette insisted on helping with the dishes. When they were finished, she asked, "Ceretha, cain't you get yo' treasures out agin? I don't reckon I ever'll get enough of seein' them an' hearin' you tell about New Hope an' that school on the hill."

"I don't think, Ceretha ever gets enough either, Bernadette. It's too hot at this time of the day to do much else. I think it would be a good idea for you to pull the chest out into the parlor and play there."

Once they succeeded in getting the chest from the bedroom to the center of the living room floor, they sat cross-legged on the floor to explore its contents. Out came Belinda, the pink calico doll that had been Mama's. Ceretha had learned to love her when she was a toddler.

"I have to be extra careful with Belinda these days," she explained, as she laid the little, old rag doll on a piece of tissue paper. "Mama doesn't think she'd live through another washing."

Beside Belinda, Ceretha placed a white box on which she had printed "HANDLE WITH CARE." In the box was another treasure which had been handed from mother to daughter. Each of Rosa Lee Brown's daughters had played with and cherished her old-fashioned china tea set. In fact, there had been quite a quarrel after Ruth Ann began house-keeping.

"One time when Ruthie came home on a visit, she wanted to take this tea set. She said it was an 'air-loom' or something—anyhow it meant something precious—and she thought she ought to be allowed to keep it."

"It's too pretty to play with," Bernadette declared.

"I seldom take all of the pieces out of the box. Mama says when I grow up, she'll divide them between Ruthie and me."

"I ain't gonna touch 'em m'self. I'd be sure as fate to drop one."

There was a dog collar, its owner had been killed on the Vicksburg Highway, and inside one of Ruth Ann's wedding announcements was a scrap of blue ribbon.

"Ruthie was all dressed for her wedding when Aunt Irene asked if she was wearing something blue. Mama couldn't find a thing, but Aunt Irene always carried just about everything in her big, old pocketbook. She pinned this piece of ribbon to Ruthie's petticoat. I'm going to wear it, too, when I get married."

The next treasure was well swathed in tissue and quite an odd shape.

"I don't 'member that one," Bernadette said.

"These I'll keep till my dying day." Ceretha sighed dramatically. The package held a pair of pink ballet slippers. Ceretha sat on the floor dangling them by their ribbons.

"Them's dancin' shoes, ain't they?"

"Ballet slippers."

"You take that kinda dancin'?"

"I've never really taken lessons. Mama let me get these for a play we had at school last spring. I was the fairy queen. Mama made my costume. One day I'll put it on and show you the dance I made up."

"Did you have your picture took?"

"Oh, yes. It's in the scrapbook. We didn't finish looking at it the other day, did we?"

Ceretha delved into the chest and brought out a wooden scrapbook. Ruth Ann had had the book especially made for her. The cover read: BROWN RABBIT, HER STORY. Mama and Ceretha had spent many, many hours finding, arranging, and pasting in the things which made up the book.

Bernadette moved closer to Ceretha so that each of them might hold one side. "We can just skip my baby pictures. I would never have won a beauty contest."

"Me, either," Bernadette snickered. "Where was you going in this pitcher?"

"To school. My very first day. Papa bought me a new lunch box. Ruthie started to college that year. She really didn't want me tagging along behind her, but the lab school was on the college campus, so I went skipping along."

Bernadette was still there when Ruth Ann stopped by on her way from work. Ceretha could hear Ruthie and Mama talking in the kitchen. Mama asked Ruth Ann to stay for supper, since Bert was working until midnight. Ruth's answer was not distinct. Ever since she had heard Ruth enter the house, Ceretha had been wrestling with a problem. Ruth did not like Bernadette. Ceretha looked at her new friend for a second, and then she took her by the hand. "I want you to meet my sister," she said.

Ruth and Mama were sitting across the table from each other, chatting. Ceretha waited politely until they seemed to have reached a break in their conversation. Her introduction was extremely dignified.

"Bernadette, this is my sister, Mrs. Logan. Ruthie, this is Bernadette, my friend."

4

A **day or so** after her formal introduction to Ruth Ann, Bernadette tapped lightly at the Browns' door. "Mornin' Miz Brown."

"Good morning, Bernadette. How nice you look. Are you coming from or going to church?"

"I been already. Mother Dear's off today. We goin' to put my school clothes in the layaway. I jes' wanted to tell Ceretha I cain't play tell evenin', maybe."

"Ceretha's a lazybones this morning. She and I sat up late last night looking at a television program. I'll tell her that you have been by. Have a

46

good time on your shopping trip."

About midmorning, Mama suggested that Ceretha take her jump rope and go out in the front to play. If Ceretha was slower than usual finding the rope, Mama didn't seem to notice. There were any number of things she found she had to do before she finally slammed the door.

"Mama," she said, as she stood with her face pressed against the screen, "I'm going to miss Bernadette today."

"Yes, dear," Mama replied in a tone that sounded as if she had thoughts of her own that were more important, for the moment at least.

Ceretha waited a moment or two hoping that she had interpreted Mama's tone incorrectly, then she sauntered out to the street. There were some children playing hopscotch in front of the tailor shop. She stood there, beside the building, for a little while, but nobody asked her to join the game. There were only a few houses between the tailor shop and the corner on the south, so she decided to venture down the block toward the church.

She hadn't skipped many feet when a boy barely missed bumping her with a bicycle. It was a girl's bike; he jumped down and stood straddling it.

"Pardon me," he said politely, "I didn't mean to hit you."

"That's all right. You didn't really hit me, just scared me."

Back and forth she went from the church to her house and from her house to the church. Occasionally, she passed the boy on the bike. He seemed to be riding around the square. They called them squares at home, but Bernadette said people here called them blocks. The boy would smile each time he passed. He was chubby, about seven or eight. His nose turned up at the end, and his eyes practically disappeared when he smiled. The next time they approached each other he stopped suddenly. If she had been skipping fast, she might have lost her balance.

"Say!" he said, "You're new around here, aren't you?"

"Uh huh," Ceretha answered shyly.

"Well, what's your name? Mine's Randall, but they call me Stuffy."

"I'm Ceretha Jane Brown."

"Ceretha? That's a new one. Course, my whole name's Randall Neil Smith. I like Stuff better, though." He smiled broadly.

During this conversation, Stuffy's sister Barbara Jean and her friend Marlene were watching from the Smiths's porch. Babs and Marlene were having a game of Jacks. Barbara checked Marlene for failing to touch the ground before starting her In-Hand Fastees.

"I was listening to Stuffy," Marlene said, "he'll make friends with anybody."

"Yeah! Daddy says Stuffy ought to make a good businessman," Babs replied.

"Maybe! I wasn't thinking of that, though," was Marlene's retort.

"Well, what are you talking about?"

"Stuffy's a boy and that makes a difference, but he doesn't know a thing about that girl, and there he is jawing away with her like she was his long lost cousin."

"What's wrong with that? At least she's nice and clean."

"The point, Babs, is *who* is she?"

"Aw!" Barbara grumbled, as she picked up the jacks once more. But Marlene hadn't finished. She was an officious child who frequently attempted to force her point of view upon her friends, and in many instances, succeeded.

"Look at it like this, Babs, you know and I know that this is not a very good neighborhood."

"We live here," Barbara snapped.

"Only because our grandparents bought these houses long before the neighborhood got so bad. And we're moving to Woodside Avenue just as soon as Dad can get a good bid for our house."

"What's that got to do with this girl?"

"That's precisely what I'm getting at," Marlene snorted.

"Well, I wish you'd hurry. I thought we came out here to play Jacks." Barbara tossed her braids

49

over her shoulders out of sheer boredom, but there was no stopping Marlene.

"Nobody who is really anybody is moving into this area now."

Marlene was actually repeating word for word part of a conversation her mother had held with a friend the evening before. As a matter of fact, if Marlene's friends had but known it, most of Marlene's cocksure attitude was because she repeated, parrotlike, any usable parts of her mother's conversations.

Marlene looked a great deal like her mother, except for one thing. Mrs. Wright had lovely chestnut hair; her daughter's was red, soft and fine, and refused to grow much more than a hand's length. The similarity of mother and daughter accounted for a major portion of Marlene's general behavior. Mrs. Wright was a secretary in an insurance office. She boasted endlessly about her teacher husband. She constantly reminded her daughter that they had to "uphold their position."

Barbara could think of no suitable answer to Marlene's last remark, so she suggested again that they resume their game. Marlene, feeling that she had won the battle, agreed. There was a slight argument about who was where in the game, and since they could not agree, they started all over again.

By this time, Stuffy, who was just naturally

inquisitive, and Ceretha were really finding out all about each other. Stuffy wanted to know, "Where's your dad work?"

"In the mill," Ceretha told him.

"Mine, too. Your mother work?"

"No, does yours?"

"She's a caseworker for the D.P.W."

"Who looks after you then?"

"M'gram. Her name's Mrs. Neil, that's how come I'm Randall Neil, for my dad and Gram. Say, d' you know my sister Babs?"

When Ceretha said she didn't, Stuffy pointed a short, fat finger in the direction of his home. Barbara and Marlene were deep in their game, apparently having forgotten the two on the sidewalk.

"Why don't you go over and ask 'em can you play? The other girl's Marlene Wright."

Stuffy waited. When Ceretha made no attempt to move, he said, "Oh, that's right, girls like to be introduced. Come on, I'll introduce you."

He turned his bicycle and walked beside it the few feet back to where his sister and Marlene sat. Stuffy left the bike at the head of the path that led to his home. Barbara saw them coming and touched Marlene.

"Wouldn't you know it?" she growled.

"Barbara and Marlene," Stuffy began, "here's a new girl in our block, Ceretha Brown. She doesn't know anybody, so I told her to come and play with you."

Marlene's "hello" was definitely cold. Barbara did smile weakly when she spoke. Once he had made his introductions, Stuffy left to continue his bicycling. As soon as she had spoken, Marlene picked up the jacks and turned her head. Ceretha wanted to run away just as fast as her legs could carry her. Barbara asked hesitantly, "Want to play?"

Marlene glared at Babs. Barbara remembered her mother saying something about not hurting people's feelings at her own house, and besides there was no real reason for not asking the girl to play— except Marlene. Ceretha's first impulse was to refuse, but that would be cowardly.

"Yes, thank you," she said, "I'd like to play."

Barbara made room for Ceretha beside her. Marlene kept right on scowling, but handed the ball and jacks to Ceretha. Babs asked if they weren't starting over. Marlene nodded. Ceretha extended her hand with the jacks toward Marlene. "I may not play exactly the way you do, so I'll be last. That way I'll have a chance to watch."

Marlene began the game without a word. Barbara began to feel a bit ashamed of her friend. She tried to cover up by asking Ceretha questions in rapid succession. They discussed ages and grades in school. Barbara was already ten, and they would both be entering the fifth grade in the fall. It was

Barbara who volunteered the information about Marlene. "Marlene's a year older than I am, and she'll be in the sixth grade."

At the sound of her name, Marlene missed. As she pushed the jacks toward Babs, she asked Ceretha, "You're from the South, aren't you?"

"Oh, yes!" Ceretha answered proudly.

"Then you'll be glad to attend a big school like ours," Marlene said. She looked like the cat who'd swallowed the mouse.

"Your school is big," Ceretha answered, smiling, "but ours was bigger."

Marlene was not to be outdone. Her next question was intended to crush Ceretha completely.

"I suppose you still find it strange to have the bathroom in the house?" she asked smugly.

This time Ceretha laughed. "We had water, electricity, and all of those things. Our bathroom was always in the house."

Barbara took no active part in this contest. She felt a little guilty at her inward glee over Marlene's failure to crush Ceretha. Marlene grew silent once more. She knew when she was licked. Ceretha found that she was enjoying the game in spite of Marlene's unfriendliness. Oddly enough, she won, played one more game, and left.

Ceretha was hardly out of earshot when Marlene stood up and announced, "You can play with her if you like, Barbara Jean Smith, but if you do, I certainly shan't play with you."

She straightened her shirt and shorts and marched home with her head high, as if she had suffered all the indignities she could bear. Marlene had used these tactics before. She was certain that before the day was over Babs would telephone, and when the conversation ended, she would have things her way.

Barbara was in the house before Marlene reached the sidewalk. She plopped herself down on the sofa and fumbled with a book. Her grandmother had heard the door close and came to the front of the house to see which of the children had come in.

"You and Marlene squabbling again?"

Barbara didn't answer. Mrs. Neil's hands were damp; she dried them on her apron and went right on talking.

"If you'd stick up to her one of these times instead of always runnin' after her, she'd quit treating you like that. What's the matter now?"

"Aw, nothing, Gram."

"I know better," Mrs. Neil said, drawing aside a curtain so that she could see, "Where's the girl that was settin' out there with you awhile ago?"

"Home, I guess."

"I don't believe I know her."

"She just moved around here."

"She seemed nice enough. Where's she from?"

"Ask Stuffy. He's the one that brought her."

Grandma Neil hadn't lived fifty-eight years for nothing, she was always saying. She left the window and took a seat diagonally across from Babs.

"You and Marlene fall out about that girl?"

No answer.

"I know one thing," Gram continued, "Stuffy may not be as smart as you in his books, but he don't let nobody lead him around by his nose. The sooner you quit the better."

Barbara was on the verge of tears. The bathroom was the closest refuge.

Four doors down the street, at Marlene's house, things were different. Grandmother Wright lived in her son's home. Donald, Marlene's father, was her only son and Marlene her only grandchild. Neither could do any wrong. Marlene had worked herself up to a white heat by the time she opened the back door, which was used to save wear and tear on their expensive living room rug.

Mrs. Wright was having a late cup of coffee. Marlene sat down at the table with her and began her story.

"Babs and I were playing Jacks on her steps when Stuffy comes bringing a strange girl to join in the game."

"Did Randall know the child?"

"That's just it, neither of us knew her at all."

"What did you do?"

"You know how softhearted Barbara is. She

ups and asks the girl to play. So I had to play with her. When she left, I told Babs how I felt about it and came home."

"Barbara should know better than to take up with any and everybody. Don't you even know where the girl lives?"

"Babs asked her. I didn't. She lives in back of the tailor shop up the street."

Grandmother Wright just about swallowed her teeth with her coffee, she drew in her breath so fast.

5

There **was** a tradition in the Brown family that every fifth birthday was to be celebrated in real style. This made Saturday of the third week in August an important day. Ceretha would be ten years old. Papa was working the four-to-twelve shift, and if the party was in the early afternoon, he could be there for at least a part of it.

"You only get to be two times five once in a lifetime," Papa said. "That absolutely calls for a party."

One morning, not long after Papa's "pronouncement" Mama and Ceretha sat down at the kitchen table to make their final plans.

"Wouldn't a family party save money, Mama?" Ceretha asked.

"Certainly, but Papa has said this is to be a real party, and you wouldn't want to be selfish about it, would you?"

"I was just thinking that since the twenty-fifth comes on Saturday and Ruthie is off at noon and Papa'd be home until three that maybe the four of us—"

"That would never do. What about Bernadette? And aren't you going to invite the children down the street? I never can think of that chubby boy's name —and his sister and the other girl with whom you played Jacks."

This was the ordeal Ceretha was trying to escape, but how was Mama to know. She hadn't fibbed about that morning at Barbara's. She had only left out the unpleasant things. Once since then, when Mama asked about the girls, she said they went to school for swimming on certain mornings, and that was perfectly true. She and Mama often met Stuffy on the street, and he was friendly as friendly could be.

What to do about Bernadette and Ruth Ann she just didn't know. It wouldn't be a party without Ruthie. She and Ruth had talked quite frankly about Bernadette one evening when Ceretha was having supper with her. Bert had been working the way

Papa was working that week, so the sisters had eaten alone. Ruthie mentioned Bernadette. Ceretha had been carefully avoiding her name. Naturally, Ruthie had used lots of grown-up words, but in substance it meant that Ruth could see nothing Ceretha could gain from playing with Bernadette. She was not happy about it when she saw the two together.

Mama was puzzled, but decided that Ceretha's reluctance was due to shyness and the many adjustments she had had to make lately. Having decided that for herself, Mama went right on with their plans.

"What is that boy's name, Brown Rabbit?"

"You mean Stuffy, Mama?"

"His rightful name, dear."

"Randall Smith."

Mama wrote it down, adjusted her glasses and asked, "And his sister and her friend?"

Ceretha swallowed hard. It would only make Mama feel badly if she knew the whole story. She swallowed again and said, "Barbara Smith and Marlene Wright."

Mama added Bernadette's name to the list and with her usual thoughtfulness asked, "Don't you think Randall might like to bring along a friend? A boy hates to be the only one in a group."

That Ceretha agreed was a good idea.

"Six children are about as many as we can have here comfortably. Now for refreshments."

Papa walked in as they started to talk about

food. Ceretha brightened up immediately. Papa's favorite candy was peppermint, and he set a bag of it on the table.

"Eats are the best part of any party," he said, drawing up a chair. "I'm glad I got here in time to help plan that part. Homemade ice cream, Mama?"

"We can't have Brown Rabbit's favorite, though. Strawberries are out of season."

"Nothing beats just plain old-fashioned vanilla," Papa answered quickly. "Wait a minute! We're not letting the Rabbit get in a word edgewise. Any objections so far?"

"So far so good. How about chocolate cake, Mama?"

"I knew you'd ask for that." Mama was silent for a second. "Chocolate never seems appropriate for a birthday cake to me. Tenth birthdays don't come often, so we'll have two cakes—a white one with decorations for the candles. We'll cut it last and everyone can take a piece home. The chocolate one we'll serve with ice cream."

"Don't forget the nuts and candies," Ceretha said, as she munched another peppermint. "Most everybody likes peppermint. We can get some of those lemon drops and jelly beans and—"

"Whoa!" Papa said, "Everybody'll go home with a tummyache. I haven't heard anything about baskets and favors."

"Mama and I are going shopping for the things

to make them right now. I'm so glad those nice teachers at Pleasant Hill Institute taught Mama how to make such pretty things. Wonder why they didn't teach us stuff like that at the lab school?"

"I grew up in the rurals of Georgia. Our teachers at the Institute were northern white missionaries who firmly believed 'idle hands are the devil's workshop.' They were concerned that we kept busy during the long rainy winter days after the crops were in and the canning done. Then, too, stores—even ten-cent stores—were in the big cities only. The closest one to our little hamlet was Savannah and that was miles away."

"I just love shopping in five-and-ten stores. I've made a list of things we need. To make the baskets, we need crepe paper, some yellow and some green. Now it absolutely has to be canary yellow, Mama, and a real, real delicate shade of green to go with it. Yellow's my favorite color—next to green."

"I know, but that's what you say about pink, and how many others," Mama interrupted. "We'd better get moving if we are going to get everything on our list."

"And please remember," Papa intervened, "I've got to have my dinner before three o'clock."

"The dinner's all cooked, Harve. I'll just have to fix the salad when I get back. We won't forget you. Why don't you see if you can't catch a nap while we're gone? One A.M.'s pretty late to get to

61

bed, and you were up shortly after seven."

"Never did like sleepin' in the daytime. I'll stretch out on the sofa and finish the mornin's paper."

Mama smiled, in her knowing way. That would take care of it, she thought, Papa'd be asleep in no time. And he was.

Shopping was fine fun, until Mama and Ceretha made their last stop for the day. Mama wanted a few groceries from the supermarket. As they entered the store, Ceretha saw Stuffy, Barbara, and their gram. She wished with all her might they'd leave before Mama noticed them. Mama went immediately to the fresh vegetable section. The Smiths and Mrs. Neil were buying bakery goods. From the looks of the cart which Barbara was pushing, they ought to be finished. Sure enough, she saw Mrs. Neil guide Barbara to the checkout counter.

Ceretha could breathe deeply once more. Up to this time, Stuffy had been occupied looking at the shelves. Ceretha was certain Barbara wouldn't speak, even if she noticed her. There had been several afternoons when Bernadette and she had been walking or playing and Babs had passed with Marlene; neither of them ever spoke.

Mama prodded Ceretha. "Come, dear," she said, "it's nearly two, and we have to give Papa his dinner."

There were four checkout counters. Ceretha rushed ahead of Mama without replying and stood at the end of the closest line. "Come over here, Ceretha. There are fewer people in this line." She indicated the line where the Smiths were. It wasn't herself Ceretha was protecting, but Mama. Somehow she hadn't wanted to tell Mama that she and Bernadette played only by themselves. Mama would understand and sympathize, too, but this was a problem that Ceretha wanted to work out on her own.

It would not have been like Stuffy not to turn around and look at the people in line behind him. His expression was one of sheer happiness when he saw Ceretha. "Hi, Ceretha. I know that's your Mom, but I never really met her, and she ought to meet my Gram."

"Hi! Stuffy this is my Mother. Mama, this is Stuffy, I mean Randall Smith."

Stuffy touched his grandmother with one hand and extended the other to Mrs. Brown. "I'm glad to meet you, and I want you to meet Gram."

Mrs. Neil and Mama exchanged greetings, while the clerk completed packing. "I guess you think we're not very neighborly 'round here," Gram said. "Ever since I saw your little girl on the porch, I been saying to myself that I ought to drop by and say a word of welcome. You kind of get out of the habit of neighborliness in a big city like this. Sometimes you live right next door to people, but you don't get to know them so good. Now that we've met, I'll be dropping by real soon."

While the two women were talking, Barbara had picked up one of the packages and walked to the exit. Mama and Ceretha could hear Mrs. Neil admonishing Barbara. "Barbara Jean, why didn't you speak to that child?"

"I didn't see her until I was over here."

"She's fibbin', Gram," Stuffy protested. "She saw her all right. Sometimes Babs just tries to act snooty like Marlene."

"Let me handle this, please, Stuffy," Mrs. Neil said. As they left the store, Gram was lecturing Barbara.

It seemed to Ceretha that the clerk was taking forever to total up Mama's purchases.

"Ceretha," Mama said, once they were outside. "I thought that you were a little slow when I asked you for the children's names this morning. Has something happened?"

"Nothing really happened, Mama. It's just that Barbara and Marlene aren't very friendly."

"That's not unusual, dear. Sometimes it takes a little while to make new friends." Mama shifted her packages, and the two of them walked on in silence.

Papa wondered why Brown Rabbit and Mama talked so little during dinner. Here they were getting ready for a big party, and nobody seemed the least bit excited. If he asked a question, he got an answer, and that was all. Papa knew that something

64

was wrong, but he decided to wait until after work to ask about it.

Mama was waiting up for him when he came in after midnight. "Up late, aren't you, Rosie?" he asked. Then he added quickly, "Though there's nothing I like better than coming home and finding you waiting up."

Mama smiled weakly and asked him if he was hungry. He was, as always. While he washed up, she set about preparing a sandwich and a glass of milk for him. Papa tasted the milk and the sandwich before he asked, "Somethin' on your mind, Rosie?"

"My mind and my heart, Harvey!"

"Something I can help with?"

Mama told him about the incident in the supermarket, and how Ceretha had cried herself to sleep.

Papa finished his snack, lit his pipe, and pushed his chair back from the table before he asked any more questions. He thought better with his pipe in his mouth. "Now let's analyze this a bit. Do you think the girl deliberately snubbed m' Rabbit?"

"It certainly seems so, Harvey."

Papa puffed furiously for a while. He was carefully organizing his thoughts. "You say the grandmother was cordial, and the little boy's been friendly from the very beginning."

"Randall is a very outgoing little boy."

"Hmmm. The Smith girl seemed friendly that

day when they first met?"

Mama nodded in agreement.

"And the grandmother chastised the girl then and there?"

Again, Mama nodded. She couldn't be so scientific about it; she knew how deeply hurt her Brown Rabbit was.

"Children are often cruel to each other, but then most times they solve their difficulties in time. Brown Rabbit's a good and lovable child. Those other children will come around. And there's nothing like a party to end the feud. There isn't a child that doesn't love to come to a party."

"Harve, I do hope you are right."

It was only because of Papa's persistent urging that Ceretha sent invitations to Babs and Marlene. She would rather have just asked Bernadette and Stuffy in for ice cream.

Saturday was a beautiful day. Ruth Ann rushed home from work to help Mama with the final touches. Mama was putting the last basket on the table. Ceretha was in the bathtub, and to keep Ruth from being disappointed at arriving too late to help, Mama suggested that she help Ceretha dress.

When she came out of her bath, Brown Rabbit got her first surprise of the day. On her bed was a brand new dress. Mama had said that the piqué, freshly laundered, would do very well. That was what she had expected to find laid out, instead there was a pale green cotton. Mama had made it by sewing at night after Ceretha had gone to bed. Ceretha danced a jig and held the dress up against herself in front of the mirror.

Ruth intervened. "How about putting it on? If you don't hurry, you won't be ready when your friends arrive. It's past one now, and the party is to begin at two."

"It is! Mama's the most wonderful Mama in the world, Ruthie. Did you ever see such a beautiful dress?"

"I don't believe I have. In fact, I think I'm a wee bit jealous. Mama made me pretty dresses, too, but this one beats them all. And look at the fancy petticoat. Is it new, too?"

"Goodness, no. This goes with my May Day dress."

Ruth Ann finally succeeded in getting her sister dressed, but they had to call for Mama to comb Ceretha's hair. "I guess you will have to have a little girl before you can comb hair, Ruthie."

Ruth Ann had braided and rebraided without satisfying either one of them. In a matter of seconds, Mama had two smooth braids and tied them with bows to match the dress.

Ceretha pirouetted around and around the birthday table, as Papa walked in. He applauded when she stopped.

"Beautiful!" he said.

"Me or the dress?" Ceretha asked.

"Both of you," he said as he embraced her.

"Be careful, Harve, or you'll muss her," Mama cautioned.

Ceretha was too elated to notice the scowl on Ruth's face when Bernadette arrived. She had spent the major part of the morning in a beauty shop. It was hard to believe that it was possible to turn her rough, stubby hair into such a work of art. A gleaming barrette held her topknot. Her pale blue dress was new and not too different from Ceretha's. Mother Dear had spent a large portion of that week's pay on Bernadette.

"I brought you a present," she said, as she
handed Ceretha a parcel all done up with pink paper
and ribbon.

Ceretha put the package with the unopened gifts
from her family. They were piled on an end table
by the sofa.

"I shan't open them until after I've blown out
the candles. You look very pretty, Bernadette."

"You looks awful scrumptious yo'self."

There was a knock on the door, and Mama
hurried to answer. There stood Stuffy in white dress
shirt and gray slacks. His pal, David Holmes, was
with him. Dave was as thin as Stuffy was fat, but

equally as good-natured. He didn't care so much for girls' parties, but Stuffy had convinced him he had to come to this one. Mama ushered them in. When they presented their gifts, Stuffy, laboring under great difficulty, began making excuses for Barbara. "My sister—Babs—well—she didn't feel so good. She's got an allergy, and——"

"You mean your sister can't come?" Ruth asked. No one had told her about the incident at the supermarket. "What about the Wright girl? Didn't you ask her, Ceretha?"

Ceretha stood mute. Stuffy looked at David for help, but David just shrugged his shoulders.

"Girls is—are—funny. When they are buddies and one can't go, they don't like to go one without the other. Anyhow, the present's from me and Babs. She helped me pick it out. Look at it like this—two guys is good as four girls any day, and we can eat twice as much ice cream and cake."

6

School opened on September 3, a little more than a week after Ceretha's birthday. No one talked about the party unless it could not be helped. Ruth Ann and Mama had heard the whole story about the morning on Barbara's porch. Ruth Ann was absolutely positive that if Mrs. Wright had known that Ceretha was her sister, things would have turned out differently. The Wrights and the Logans attended the same church. Ceretha pleaded with Ruth Ann not to talk with Mrs. Wright.

"If Marlene wants to be friends because she wants to, all right. But I don't want her being nice to me because her mama told her to."

Mama was glad that Ceretha chose to make it on her own.

Indications were that this first day of school was going to be warm and sunny. Ceretha wore a new plaid dress. She sat on the edge of Mama's bed, watching her put the final touches to her hair.

"Mama," she said, "I bet you can't guess what Stuffy told me the other day!"

"I doubt that I can."

"He said that Barbara lets Marlene lead her around by the nose."

"Oh!"

"And do you know what else he said? Barbara really wanted to come to my party. Her allergy was bothering her some, but she was scared to come."

"Scared to come?" Mama repeated.

"She's scared that Marlene won't play with her if she does what Marlene tells her not to do."

"Isn't that silly, dear?"

"But Marlene's her best friend, Mama."

"Oh!"

Ceretha knew from the tone of Mama's voice that she really didn't understand. There was no use trying to explain. Bernadette saved her by knocking.

"You and Miz Brown ready, Ceretha? It's getting hot outside. I wish we was still havin' vacation."

"Don't you like school, Bernadette?" Ceretha asked.

"It's all right, but I like vacation better."

"I love school. I'm kind of excited about going back."

"More than 'kind of,' judging by the small amount of breakfast you ate this morning. I hope you do better by your lunch."

"I will, Mama, and I hope that Bernadette and I have the same lunch hour. There are two lunch periods, you know."

"I'm sure that it would please the two of you to have the same lunchtime, and I hope that you do, but if you shouldn't, there must be lots of new friends to get to know at school." Mama locked the door, and the three of them started toward the Wilson Elementary School.

Ceretha and Bernadette kept up an endless line of chatter all the way to the school. Sometimes they included Mama. "Bernadette was just explaining to me," Ceretha said, "that there may be as many as three rooms of the same grade."

"They put all the smart ones in one class and so on like that, Miz Brown. I just betcha Ceretha gets in a smart class."

"I wonder which fifth grade class Barbara's in, don't you, Mama?"

"I really wasn't thinking about it, Brown Rabbit. Is that the class that you would like to be in?"

"I think so, Mama."

"There is quite a chance that you may not be.

Is it really that important? As I said a while back, in a school as large as Wilson, you should be able to make many friends."

"Las' year the chil'run in my class, they kinda go aroun' in bunches. They mostly already knowed each other. Mary Holliday, my ver' bes' friend, she move to the project and now she at Hambilton School."

"At any rate," Mama said, "both you and Ceretha will find new friends. You're both nice girls and others will want to be with you."

"Yes'um," Bernadette answered, "but it ain't alway lak grown-ups thinks."

Most of the children who were accompanied by parents were kindergartners. Transfer students were interviewed first. Mr. Tobias, the principal, examined Ceretha's records, and then said, "Mrs. Brown, your daughter comes to us with a very high scholastic record. There is also an unusual letter of recommendation from her former principal. However, it has been our experience that often students from the Deep South are not equipped to do the work required here. We have homogeneous groups in our school—that is, we put children with the same relative aptitudes and achievement together."

Mama was pleased. "I'm acquainted with homogeneous grouping, and I am certain that Ceretha can compete with the best students you have."

The principal had a son and daughter, so he

74

could understand Mama's pride. Ceretha made a mental note to look up "homogeneous."

Then she went back to listening to Mr. Tobias. "Let's see—we'll put Ceretha in the fifth grade—and in the fast-moving class. Lots of competition in this class, young lady. We'll try you there for the first marking period. If we find that she cannot keep up, Mrs. Brown, we will have to make a change."

"She'll keep up," Mama said firmly.

"Her homeroom teacher will be Mrs. Annice Hudson, one of our very best teachers. If you will give this card to Mrs. Carter, the secretary just outside my door, she will direct you to the room after she has completed the enrollment." He shook hands with Mama and assured Ceretha that she would like Wilson.

Mrs. Carter completed the enrollment forms and then asked Mama if she could pay the book-rental fee that day.

Before Mama could answer, Ceretha asked, "What is book rental?"

"Fees you pay for the use of the textbooks, dear. You don't buy your books or pay tuition here."

Mama paid the fee, and Mrs. Carter gave her a card of admittance and directions to Ceretha's room. When they reached the main corridor, Ceretha asked, "Are you going home now, Mama?"

"I thought I'd walk to your classroom with you. I'd like to meet Mrs. Hudson."

Although Ceretha was proud of her mother, she would rather have faced the class alone. Mama went right along. She and Mrs. Hudson said all the things that teachers and mothers are apt to say to each other in such instances. Mama promised to attend the monthly PTA meetings. Several children snickered or whispered loudly while Mrs. Hudson was talking with Mrs. Brown. Mrs. Hudson asked a child in the front seat nearest the blackboard to step up to the board. The girl began to write the names of the talkers on the board. After that, there was comparatively little talk.

When Mrs. Brown left the room, Mrs. Hudson put her hand on Ceretha's shoulder and guided her to the front of the room. There was something about Mrs. Hudson's touch that made Ceretha feel that she would be both a teacher and a friend.

"It's too bad," Mrs. Hudson said, "that more of your parents don't come to school with you. This school would be a much better place if we saw more of your parents.

"We have a new student, Ceretha Jane Brown. I want you to make her welcome and help her get acquainted with our school. Ceretha, there is a vacant seat in the second row. Sit there for the present."

As Ceretha walked toward her seat, she looked around for familiar faces. There were one or two she remembered having seen before. In the third seat of the fourth row, sat Barbara Smith. Ceretha smiled. Barbara leaned forward and whispered something to the girl in front of her, who turned to get a better look at Ceretha.

"Barbara Smith," Mrs. Hudson reprimanded, "If you have something of interest to say, please stand up and tell the whole class. If not, keep quiet until I give you permission to speak."

Barbara's face was red as a beet. She was a good student, well-liked by students and teachers. She fully intended to keep this reputation. Now, within the first few minutes of the first day in her new class, she had been singled out for a misdemeanor. As she sat, with her face burning, she thought, that Ceretha Brown again—always getting me into trouble.

Routine affairs occupied the first part of the period. When Mrs. Hudson finished explaining the daily schedule, which differed from the previous year in that the children would change classroom and teacher for each subject, she announced, "I am your homeroom teacher, and I will have you for language arts. Some of you I know from last year. I want to get acquainted with all of you as quickly as possible. By the end of the week, I'd like to have you divided into your reading groups. I'll begin to get some ideas today. Will George Jones, Donna Weathers, Alfred Baker, and Ceretha Brown get the books from the table in the rear of the room and pass them out."

Several children, including Barbara Smith, raised their hands. "I believe we have enough," Mrs. Hudson said, "thank you, anyway. When you have your book, turn to the first story. We will begin with row one. Each child will read until I signal to stop. Give your name, loud and clear, and begin where the reader before you left off."

Most of the children murmured "Thanks" when a book was placed on their desk. Barbara did not even look up when Ceretha put a nice, new, and shiny book in front of her. Ceretha had chosen an especially clean book for her as a gesture of friendship.

A crisp "That will do," told most pupils when to stop reading. If the child read exceptionally well, or very poorly, Mrs. Hudson would make some specific comment, such as, "That sounded as if you really understood what you were reading." Or she would say, "Word, words, nothing but words, you will have to work harder."

Ceretha hoped that she would get a chance to read before the hour was up. She was confident that she read well. When her name was called, she stood straight and tall beside her seat and read with assurance. Instead of saying, "That will do!" Mrs. Hudson said, "You read very well, Ceretha. Make certain that you keep up the good work."

The bell sounded for the next class. Althea Bond, who sat in front of Ceretha, offered to show her around for the rest of the day. "Sometimes I almost get lost myself. I came to Wilson from Jersey City last year. Even though the class is supposed to stay together, there's so many kids going so many different ways at the same time, it gets mixed up. You read good, girl, 'cause when Mrs. Hudson says you're good, you're super. Lots of kids say she's mean, but she ain't. She don't take no foolishness though. If you're looking for a mean teacher, this Mrs. Cole we're going to right now's a mean one."

Althea stopped for breath for the first time. As they went inside the door, Ceretha asked, "Is she really mean or just cross sometimes?"

"Wait and see. She's jes' plain mean."

The moment the bell rang, Mrs. Cole rapped on her desk with a ruler. "This is an arithmetic class and not a gabfest. I expect you to pay strict attention at all times, and I will accept nothing less."

Althea shot a quick glance at Ceretha, as if to say, "I told you so!" That hour passed very quickly. Mrs. Cole gave them a series of brief review tests on concepts in new math, which had been introduced the previous year. The children checked each other's papers, but there was no unnecessary talking. Barbara and a boy named Marcus were the only ones who made perfect scores. Ceretha told Althea, as they left the room, "I'm going to have to get my brother-in-law to help me with this new math. We just had a little of it second semester last year."

"New math, old math, it's all the same to me. I'll do good to make a D. We need recess after that class. Come on, girl. We got fifteen minutes on the playground. No use trying for the swings. Certain kids break their necks every day to get to them. One of my friends brings a big jump rope or else my bunch, we just set somewhere and talk. If you ain't got no certain chum, you might as well come along. Otherwise, you might be standin' out there alone, 'cause some kids is funny about talking to other kids they don't know."

"I know," Ceretha managed to say.

"I never was like that, though. When I see a

new kid, I figure, well gee, that kid might be lonesome or something, and so I always go right up to the kid and start talking. Look, there's Betty and the rest of 'em over by the double gates. They don't never open them gates. Come on, let's hurry."

"Can you wait just one minute?"

"Didja see somebody you know?"

"No, but I've a friend in the fourth grade. I'd like to look for her."

"Go here last year? What's her name?" Althea asked, but did not wait for an answer. "Gee, kid, you might as well come on with me. Maybe you'll see this kid and maybe you won't. What'd you say her name was?"

"Bernadette Hughes."

"Never heard of her. Like I say, you can watch for her while you're jumping rope."

It was easier to go with Althea than to listen to her endless chatter if Ceretha had attempted to argue. Althea introduced Ceretha to her friends. Those who had not seen each other during the summer exchanged experiences for a while, and then the game of rope really got under way. There was no time during the game that Althea was quiet. Occasionally, one of her friends would remark that she talked too much, but that didn't bother Althea. She laughed and went right on talking.

Ceretha was constantly on the lookout for Bernadette, because she was sure that if Bernadette was out for recess at this time she would be watching for her. Toward the end of the period, Ceretha saw Bernadette playing Tag with a group. Ceretha excused herself with difficulty, for Althea intervened. "Gosh, kid," she said, "recess is almost over, and your girl friend's busy playing with other kids. We can sorta keep an eye on her, and you can speak to her on the way into the building. After all, I gotta show you the way around. You don't know the way to the science class, now do you?"

Ceretha agreed that she did not, but she said, "I can find you easier than I can watch for Bernadette. You're jumping rope here, and she's running all over the place. I'll be right back in one second." She did not give Althea time to reply, but began making her way toward the place where she had last seen Bernadette. She found her without too much trouble. It was impossible to tell which was happier, Bernadette or Ceretha.

"Gracious, chile," Bernadette cried. "I look all over this playgroun' fuh you."

"And I've been looking for you, too. One of the girls in my class is helping me find my way around, and I've been playing with her."

"From now on, les meet right by the wes' door. You got first or second lunch?"

"We have the second. What about you?"

"Shuckins! We first! Now ain't that too bad!"

"Well, we can walk home together. I'll meet

you at the west door. I'd better get back to Althea. I haven't the slightest idea where to find the next class."

Bernadette walked part of the way across the playground with Ceretha. She felt just a trifle jealous of Ceretha's dependence upon her classmate and wished that she had made fifth grade, then she'd be showing Ceretha around.

Althea greeted Ceretha's return with her usual glibness. "So you found your chum okay. Why didn't you bring her over here with you? The more the merrier I say. Ever play Double Dutch? That's what we're going to play now. Not today, though, there goes the bell."

7

In the days immediately following the opening of school, the keen rivalry for scholastic achievement between Barbara and Ceretha became more and more evident. Both girls were hard-working students and vied with each other at every opportunity. Each had a silent cheering section in the room. Only Marcus Lawless took no part. Marcus had had top honors in the fourth grade, with Barbara a very close second. He did not intend to be unseated by either of the girls.

This fall, for the first time, French was being taught twice a week to the fifth graders. Ceretha enjoyed this new experience.

One warm afternoon, after school, Ceretha was sitting on the back steps of the apartment building going over her French dialogues. Bernadette came racing around the house and stood listening to her friend. Ceretha acted as if she didn't know Bernadette was there.

"You talkin' to yo'se'f, Ceretha?"

"I'm studying my French," was the crisp reply.

"It's too hot to study, and besides we jes' come from school. You lak French?"

"Yes, and I wish you'd let me study."

"Say sumpthin' in French. Back home in Louisiana some folks talks French. In the parish where Mother Dear comes from, lots of folks talks it. They sounds so funny. Mother Dear know some words, but she cain't talk it good. Say sumpthin', Ceretha."

"I can say 'close your mouth!' "

"Say that then. I jes' want to hear you talk French."

"Bernadette, sometimes you are so thick-headed. I said I was—"

Mama interrupted from the kitchen. "Ceretha!"

"Yes, Mama?"

"Was that necessary?"

"I'm sorry, Bernadette, but—"

This time Bernadette interrupted, "That's okay, I wuz jes' goin' to axe you to go some place with me."

85

Again, Mama spoke from inside, "It might not be a bad idea to relax a little, dear. I thought I was to have a French lesson after supper, anyway."

"All right, Mama. As the kids at school say, 'if you can't lick 'em, join 'em.' Where do you want to go, Bernadette?"

"Over to Wickham House. It's time to sign up."

"Sign up? For what?"

"Mos'ly fuh to play. 'Cose there are other things you can do, like join clubs an' things."

"Do they have a library?"

"Naw, but the liberry ain't fur from Wickham, though. I don't lak to read much."

"I do. I love to read. Is there a Girl Scout troop at Wickham House?"

"I'm mos' certain they has one."

"*Have* one, Bernadette," Ceretha corrected sharply. "I'm sorry—I'm peeved. I only got a B on my French conversation today, and there were A's."

"Shuckins. B's a plenty good mark. Les' go! You can study French after a while."

Ceretha went inside to talk to Mama. Bernadette sat down on the steps to wait. "I have to be home by five-thirty. Let's go to the library first. I want to get a card. Are you going to get one, too?"

"I'll get one 'cause our teacher say evabody oughta have a liberry card."

At the library, Ceretha and Bernadette were

86

given applications which had to be signed by a parent before they could take books home.

"I'll tell Mama how to find the library, and she'll bring my application back tomorrow while we're at school. Mama'll probably get an adult card, because next to sewing, she likes reading."

"Reckon she'll bring mine back, ef Mother Dear signs it tonight?"

"Of course, she will, silly. Look, we're back on Mount Vernon Street already. I thought—"

"I'll beat cha to Wickham House!" Bernadette challenged, and took off immediately.

"I wouldn't want to have to run track against you, Bernadette," Ceretha said, breathlessly, when she caught up with her friend at the door.

They were greeted by Natascha Brailowsky, who taught folk and modern dancing, but was substituting for the regular intake person. "Nat," as the children called her, was elated to see Bernadette. "Why, hello, Bernadette! Did you have a good summer? We didn't see you at day camp. And who is your friend?"

"Hullo, Miss Nat." Bernadette was not yet free enough in her relationships with white people not to accord them special titles. At home, in Louisiana, no Negro would think of talking to a white person without saying, "Sir," or "Mam." Even though other children attending Wickham House always greeted Natascha as "Nat," Bernadette was uncomfortable trying to do so.

"This here's Ceretha Brown," Bernadette stammered.

"I'm happy to meet you, Ceretha. Just call me Nat, Natascha Brailowsky is much too long."

Nat's smile was genuine, and Ceretha, who had encountered race prejudice, but also had come in contact with people like Nat before, smiled back.

She gave the girls registration forms to fill out, and when that was done, she gave them each a list of possible activities from which they were to choose.

"This year, Bernadette, I hope you are going to sign up for one of my dancing classes."

"No'm, Miss Nat! You know I cain't dance. I jes' wuzn't cut out fur dancing."

"I love to dance," Ceretha piped up, "May I join the class?"

"There are several dance groups. I'd like to have you join one or more of them. When you've made your choices, see if you can't get Bernadette to come with you."

Ceretha and Bernadette went to a table where other children were signing up. Occasionally one of them would leave the table and ask Nat a question.

"There certainly are a lot of things you can do here," Ceretha said. "I hardly know which to choose. I see so many things I'd like to do. Did you belong to any of the clubs last year, Bernadette?"

"Naw, I mos'ly jes' lak the playroom. They's

got mos' nigh the prettiest dollhouse in the whole world. All kinds of dolls, an' dishes, and curtains at the winders—jes' lak real."

"But you ought to belong to something. What have you marked on your list?"

"Nothin' yet. I'm still thinkin'."

"Let's do it together then. How about art?"

"I cain't draw none."

They went down the list together. Ceretha reading, while Bernadette indicated whether she was interested. Under the heading of dancing, there were several subdivisions, including folk and square dancing; tap and modern interpretive. Ceretha thought that she understood the latter, but she went to Nat to make certain. When she came back to the table, she said to Bernadette, "You just listen to music and then do what it makes you feel or see. I'd like to take that and tap and folk dancing, too, but I just know that Mama's not going to let me come here every day."

"Las' yeah I use to come evaday, but 'taint no sense in me joinin' no dancin' class, Ceretha."

"If Mama let's me come, please come with me."

Bernadette reluctantly made a check on her list where she had seen Ceretha check hers. Brownie Scouts and Girl Scouts were listed and that made Ceretha very happy. She asked the other girls at the table about the age limits. She and Bernadette were the right age for Junior Girl Scouts. When Ceretha had convinced Bernadette that they both ought to

89

join, one of the children at the table said, "Won't do you no good to sign up for Girl Scouts. Both troops is full up. You can ask Nat, though, an' make sure."

Nat told her that scouting was so popular that both of the troops had more than their quotas, plus long waiting lists. "We'll take your name, though," she added.

"I've waited my whole life to get to be a Girl Scout. In New Hope, we didn't have a Negro Brownie troop, so I wasn't a Brownie. Now it looks like I won't be a Girl Scout, either. Thank you, anyway."

Nat was disturbed by Ceretha's intense disappointment. She leafed through the pile of registration forms until she found hers. She wanted to know more about Ceretha. The answers might give some clues as to her background. All these things, and more, went through Nat's mind as she studied Ceretha's questionnaire. She became so engrossed in her analysis that she did not see the regular intake clerk when she reported for duty.

Betty Miles watched Nat for a moment, then laughed. "Now, Nat, I know that I have the most exciting job in the whole agency, but I am not going to let you have it."

"Sorry, I didn't hear or see you, Betty. You're joking about your job, but it can be a pretty interesting one."

"If you had it every evening from six until ten, five days a week, you might not think so."

"I don't know. I might try it for a while; just to get the feel of it. But I found it interesting for the short time I had to relieve you.

"Look, Betty, do me a favor, please. See the girl in the blue plaid dress, or better still, do you remember Bernadette?"

"Who doesn't? That child is a comical character."

"I disagree. When the girl sitting next to Bernadette brings you her Interest Finder, hold her here until I come back. I'm going to see if I can get her into a scout troop."

"You know as well as I do that both of our troops are full and running over. Now, if she wanted to be a Cadette, she might have a bit of a chance, but she doesn't look as if she is old enough for Cadettes."

"I've known Clara to take in another Junior or two when the need was pressing. I wouldn't even ask Mabel; she is a conformist."

"This time I don't think she'll do it. Most of the kids in her troop flew up last spring. She won't have many dropouts. And how about the others on the waiting list?"

"I know all that, but I feel compelled to try."

Betty Miles shook her head in disbelief. She liked her work, and she liked order. Nat had left the desk in disarray. She was restoring her desk to order when someone tapped her lightly on the shoulder. It was Bernadette, with Ceretha beside her.

"Howdy do Miz Miles. Miss Nat gone?"

"Good evening, Bernadette. Is your friend's name Ceretha? Nat wanted you girls to wait for her. She'll be back in a few minutes. Have you shown Ceretha the rest of the House?"

"No'm. I was thinkin' about it, though."

"Then why don't you go now? By the time you've finished, Nat should be back."

Betty studied the two girls as they walked away. The new one is nice and clean, she thought, but other than that I don't see anything so special about her.

Bernadette took Ceretha to see the dollhouse first. Papa would have done a much better job on the furniture, Ceretha thought, but she was too polite to say so. The playroom, clubrooms for the Golden Agers, the nursery school, and business offices made up the ground floor. They toured the second and third floors and the gymnasium. As they approached Mrs. Miles's desk again, Bernadette explained that the fourth floor had special conference rooms and that some of the staff lived next door in a wing which had been built much later than the original building.

They had to wait a few minutes before Nat returned. She walked toward them slowly. "Been waiting long? Sorry, but I wanted to see what I could do to get Ceretha into a Girl Scout troop. It simply can't be done at this time, but Miss Carson says that there is a small troop at St. Mark's Episcopal Church. You may be able to get in there. Have your mother call Mrs. Kigh at this number." Nat handed Ceretha a slip of paper on which a telephone number was written. "Now, did either of you sign up for dancing? I'll be disappointed if you didn't."

"We both did," Ceretha answered, "the modern dance class and the folk dance class. Maybe Mama will let me come to both."

On the way home, Ceretha and Bernadette swung along hand in hand. "I like Nat," Ceretha said.

"I like Miss Nat, too," Bernadette echoed.

"Nat's what Bert calls 'my kind of people.' "

"White people you mean?"

"No, silly! Just people that you like real, real well—any-color people. Do any white children go to Wickham House?"

"Now who's silly? Ain't no white childrun live in this neighborhood. Why you axe?"

Ceretha was slow in responding. "Nothing! I was just wondering—Ruthie keeps talking—forget it. Look over there." She pointed toward the other side of the street. "There are Marlene, Barbara, Celestine, and Yvonne. You know what? Marlene belongs to St. Mark's, maybe she knows about the Girl Scouts there. She might even be one."

"Well I sho' wouldn't be axing her 'bout it, if I wuz you."

"Well, you aren't me, and I'm going to ask her."

"Go 'head! I'm goin' to stay on this side of the street tell I get right across from our house."

"Oh, Bernadette, that's silly. Come on, let's cross here. You don't have to say a word."

"An' I ain't either."

Marlene was the first to see the pair approaching. She punched Barbara and said, "Here comes your friend Ceretha, Babs."

"She's not my friend, and you know it," Barbara snorted. Celestine, who was waiting for her father to pick her up, turned toward Marlene and asked, "What have you got against her?"

Since she had no real answer, Marlene played the role of the superior authority, "If you don't know, Celestine, I certainly shan't enlighten you."

"Don't then. Looks like they're coming over here."

Ceretha greeted the girls, but Bernadette walked a few steps beyond the group and stopped.

"Marlene," Ceretha said, "I really came to ask you a question." There was no response from Marlene, but Ceretha went on. "I want to be a Girl Scout, and I understand that there may be room in the troop at St. Mark's. Do you belong to the troop?"

"And if I do?" Marlene asked with a sneer.

"And if you do," Ceretha mimicked, "you

certainly don't know the rules of the game. I believe there is a Girl Scout law which says 'A Girl Scout is courteous.'" Then she turned and walked away.

8

Ceretha told Mama as soon as she got home. "I don't think Marlene's friends were proud of her," Mama commented.

Then she called Mrs. Kigh about the scout troop, only to be told, "We have only one leader and that keeps our troop small. We prefer to take girls from our own parish first, then if there are vacancies, we take other girls. We will put your child's name on the waiting list."

Disappointment over the Girl Scout troop gradually subsided under a deluge of exciting things that were happening or about to happen. Saturday had become the day to live for, primarily because of Nat's modern dancing class. Mama had gone to Wickham House to meet this wonderful person who was beginning to mean so much to Ceretha. At school, everything was going very well. Ceretha was mastering the French, and it was great fun. Bert's help with the new math was invaluable. In fact, one Saturday afternoon, Ceretha said to Mama, "Life's wonderful!"

"I'm glad to hear it." Mama was making a cake for Sunday dinner. Ceretha was perched on her bright red stool, watching and hoping that Mama would make a sample. Sometimes Mama baked a tiny cake first in one of Ceretha's old toy pans. If she could withstand the delicious aroma of the big cake, Ceretha would save her sample and frost it with Mama's finished cake. Often the little cake was eaten while it was still warm. Mama tested her mixture and then asked, "Anything in particular making life so wonderful, Brown Rabbit?"

"Millions of things, Mama!"

"Millions, dear?"

"Well, lots and lots of them, anyhow."

"For example?"

"First take today. When Papa comes home at five, he doesn't go back to work until Monday at three. Isn't that wonderful?"

97

"It will be nice to have Papa home. Here lately he's been working so hard that he's had to sleep a great deal more. What else?"

"Bert's off Sunday, too, Ruth said. Maybe he'll take the whole family for a long ride in the jalopy. He promised he would the first chance he got."

"You must remember, though, that Ruth and Bertram have their own friends and plans."

"Oh, I wasn't going to ask, Mama. I was just hoping."

"Is that all of your wonderful list?"

"Goodness, no!"

Mama went to the cupboard and came back with the sample pan.

"I was sitting here with my fingers and toes crossed hoping you wouldn't forget the sample! Nat's going to have a surprise for the person who makes up the best dance to 'Clair de Lune.'"

"Clara do what?"

"Not Clara, Mama. It's a piece about moonlight, and that's French for moonlight, I guess. Anyway, that's the way Nat pronounced it. I've got a swell idea."

"How is Bernadette getting along with dancing?"

"Oh, Mama, she's the funniest thing. She's right when she says she can't dance. Julia says that Bernadette has two left feet."

"Who is Julia?"

"Don't you remember, Mama. She's the girl in my Sunday school class who lives in the next block. Bernadette, Julia, and I walk to school together some mornings, but Julia's real pokey, so sometimes we go on without her. Did I tell you that her mother is president of one of the ladies' circles at church. Julia thinks you two would like each other."

"What's her mother's name? I would like to meet her."

"Mrs. Butler. I don't know her first name. You'd like Julia. She says the funniest things. I'll call her right now and tell her to stay for church tomorrow so that you can meet her and her mother."

"I'd like that. I'm glad that you are finding new playmates."

"Bernadette's still my very best friend and Julia's second best. We're both working on Bernadette and her speech. Sometimes she makes me so mad. I tell her the same thing over and over again."

"I have been wanting to speak to you about that. I noticed that lately you are often very impatient with her."

"But, Mama, sometimes I think she doesn't even try."

"How good would your speech be, Brown Rabbit, if you had spent the first eight or nine years of your life somewhere where you had only six or seven months of the poorest kind of schooling?"

"I'll try to remember, Mama."

Mama was still in the kitchen when Papa came home from work. Ceretha was sprawled on the living room floor chatting with Julia over the telephone. When she heard Papa's voice, she quickly ended her conversation. Papa looked tired. He missed every day in the sunshine, the sight of green things growing, and the leisure to whittle. He tried, as best he could, to carry on little things that had made life easier in New Hope. On Saturday evening, he had always brought home a surprise. For two Saturdays now, he had missed bringing anything, and it bothered him. Last week he had been on the night shift, and he had slept the better part of the day. The week before he had gone with Bert to look at a house Bert was interested in, and they had overstayed their time.

"Guess," he said, holding a bag beyond Ceretha's reach.

"Peppermint!"

"In a bag this big? Guess again!"

"Peaches, then." She remembered having heard Mama say that she had looked for a certain kind of peach and couldn't find it.

"If you miss this time, it's Mama's turn."

"Wait now! Not peaches and not peppermint. Must be—give me a hint, Papa."

"Begins with a 'g,' and we haven't had any for ages."

"I should have known it was grapes."

"Wrong again. Are you going to guess, Rosie?"

"I was going to say grapes, Harve. You'll have to tell us."

"Good old-fashioned ginger cookies. I walked from the mill almost to Tenth Street. Needed the exercise and the sunlight. I saw these cookies in a bakery. They reminded me of home, and I bought some. I didn't forget those other Saturdays. Time just gets away from me these days."

"You're always thoughtful, Harve," Mama said, and she kissed him on his forehead. "Wash up for supper now."

Papa left the table the minute supper was over. He wanted to get into the living room, where he could stretch his legs. Brown Rabbit brought his slippers and put the footstool under his feet. Then she and Mama cleared the table and washed the dishes.

When Ceretha and Mama joined Papa in the living room, he was napping. Ceretha signaled to Mama to tiptoe, but a creaking board in the floor awakened Papa.

"Ah, he said, caught you in the act. Get the Good Book, 'lil Rabbit. We haven't read our Sunday school lesson."

Every Saturday, since Ceretha could recall, the family had gone over the Scripture for the next day's lesson. At first, Ruthie or Mama had read the lesson. Papa always led the discussion. When Brown

Rabbit learned to read well enough, she read, with Mama helping her with the hard words.

This night she took the big family Bible from the top of the bookcase and sat on a hassock near Papa. Papa had already been reading from the Presbyterian lesson book. It was on the floor beside the sofa.

"Luke, the eleventh chapter, the first through the thirteenth verses."

Mama had her Testament so that she could follow more easily. Ceretha found the place and began to read. Papa puffed steadily on his pipe through the first six verses, then he dropped off to sleep again. Ceretha read on through the thirteenth verse. Just as she closed the book, Papa awakened.

"There," he said, "is the crux of the problem. 'Lord teach us to pray.' Listen well to your teacher tomorrow, little Rabbit."

He was about to fall asleep again, but Mama urged him to go to bed.

Ceretha and Mama had a slight disagreement over what she would wear to Sunday school. Once that was settled, it wasn't long before Mama told Ceretha to get ready for bed.

"If you stay up late looking at television, you aren't going to want to get up in time for Sunday school."

Ceretha wheedled for just one extra half hour. There was a good animal act on TV.

After Sunday school, the next morning, Ceretha told Julia that her mother and father were both in church. "Papa," she said, "comes in time for the adult Bible class. Mama says that Papa missed his calling—he should have been a preacher. I told them where to meet us."

Julia checked the time by her new wristwatch, and the two girls hurried up the stairs. Mrs. Butler was already in the process of introducing herself to the Browns. Since there were only the three of them in the entryway, she had no difficulty deciding that the couple must be Mr. and Mrs. Brown.

"I'm Chessie Butler. I've been coming here for so many years that I can usually spot newcomers right off. I've met Ceretha; she seems such a nice child."

When Ceretha and Julia appeared, she said, "I've already introduced myself to your parents. We can sit together, if you would like. I believe we are in time for the organ prelude."

"We'd like that, Mrs. Butler," Papa volunteered for his family. "Does your husband attend First Presbyterian also?"

"Yes, but he is working today."

"That's one thing I don't like about this mill work—no respect for the Lord's day," Papa said.

Ceretha nudged Julia as they followed their parents into the sanctuary. Julia looked up at Papa and smiled knowingly. After services, Mrs. Butler made Mama acquainted with several members of her Circle. Mama promised to attend the very next meeting which was being held at the Butler home.

The Logans were home from church before the Browns. Bert kept his promise of the ride without any one reminding him. Ruth Ann suggested that they plan a picnic before the last of the warm weather was gone. That gave Ceretha another item for her "wonderful list."

She had to wait until the last class hour on Monday for the wonder event of that day.

Other teachers in the art department insisted that Wanda Goodwin, Ceretha's art teacher, sat up all night, every night, thinking up projects with which to inspire her pupils. No other grade school art teacher at Wilson was able to get such unusually good work from her classes. Miss Goodwin did give lots of time and thought to her planning. In addition, she thoroughly enjoyed working with the children. She had promised her classes that for the month of October they might work on materials for a Halloween party.

Ceretha's class was teaming with excitement. Althea, whom Miss Goodwin had nicknamed, "The Bubbler," started the period with, "Come on Miss Goodwin, tell us about the party. We've been bragging about it all over the school. A girl in class thirty-seven said you were going to let them have one, too. Ours has got to be the best."

Miss Goodwin clamped her hand over Althea's mouth so that she could no longer talk.

"I promised you a party IF, capitalized and underscored, IF you planned it. I was so sure that you'd come in with it all mapped out that I spent the weekend in the country thinking what an easy job I'd have if every class was like fifty-four. Now just look at you; nobody has an idea.

"I'll give you five minutes to think. This is an art class, and we are going to spend the next four weeks getting ready for a party. Put your thinking caps on. Ready. Go."

She didn't have to enforce silence. She stood against her desk smiling at the intent faces, the scratching of heads, and the chewing of pencils. This is a nice class, and a bright one, she thought. This group ought to be a good one for puppetry. Maybe we can have a puppet play for our auditorium program.

"Time's up. I'll write the ideas we accept on the blackboard. Barbara Smith, your hand was up first."

"Invitations ought to come first."

"No argument there, I'm sure. Now Ceretha, before you shake off your arm."

"Decorations would be next."

The suggestions came thick and fast for the next few minutes. They decided to make favors, masks, and there was time to design their own costumes.

"See what you can do when you apply yourselves. We've time to choose the various committees before the bell rings. If we work in small groups on everything except the masks and costumes, we'll get done faster."

"Two groups of eleven and one of ten should do nicely—invitations, decorations, and favors. Each group may elect its own chairman."

Barbara decided to switch from invitations to decorations, since there were more children who volunteered for the first group. That put her on the committee with Ceretha. Miss Goodwin gave them permission to gather in different parts of the room for their elections.

Althea had never ceased being Ceretha's self-appointed guardian, so naturally when Ceretha made a choice, Althea's was the same.

"The Bubbler" enjoyed a certain popularity because of, and in spite of, her eternal bubbling, so some of her friends joined the decorations group. Althea also loved a good scrap, verbal or physical, and she knew how to start one.

"I nominate Ceretha for chairman," she said, without waiting for anyone to call the group to order.

Babs had a friend or two in the group, too, and Donna Weathers nominated her. Ceretha won.

"You only won by one vote," Barbara chided Ceretha.

"But, I won," Ceretha rebutted.

9

By the middle of October, the Brown family knew that a part of their daily routine was to listen to the progress being made on the Halloween party.

One evening Mama decided to attend a lecture for parents at the settlement house, but she did not want to take Ceretha with her, so Ruth Ann said she would enjoy having Ceretha spend the evening with her. "It has been such a long time since we had a real chat, and I get terribly lonesome when Bert works this shift."

Ceretha took some crayons and paper with her, because she wanted to get a head start on a design for her mask. They were to begin the actual making of them the next afternoon. The two sisters sat in silence for sometime, Ruth with a book and Ceretha with her sketching.

Then suddenly Ceretha turned toward Ruth and said, "I like your apartment, Ruthie. I wish we could at least move to the front of the house."

"Having a view to the street helps some, but there's very little worth looking at."

"Yes, but even though it's almost dark now, this room looks pretty."

"There are several reasons for that. The front windows face west, so we get the late sun. Bert and I planned this room carefully so that it would help us forget some of the sordidness outside."

"What's sordidness?"

"I guess the simplest way to explain it is to say it's just another word for ugliness."

"Oh! Want to see the sketch I've made?"

"I certainly do, and I haven't been brought up to date on the party. How did your committee work out?"

"Swell. We've finished making all of the decorations, but we haven't put them up. We're saving some until the day before the party."

"Did Babs help?"

"Not very much, but nearly all the other kids worked extra hard, so it didn't matter. Miss Goodwin caught Babs doing nothing the other day and told her that she'd spoil her grade by loafing. She worked the rest of that period. Here's my mask. I wanted to put the red in before I showed it to you."

Ruth Ann looked at two rough sketches showing impish looking faces, with long noses and pointed ears. She studied them for a while, then asked, "What on earth is it?"

"It's an elf's face. Doesn't it look like one?"

"Well, I suppose it does. Why an elf? And how will you ever make it?"

"Our masks are supposed to fit in with our costumes. I want to be an elf like Jack Frost. I've already decided how I want my costume made, but I haven't drawn it yet."

"It's the long nose and the big ears that worry me. I can't see how you are going to make them."

"I don't exactly know myself. Miss Goodwin told us we'd use cheesecloth and strips of gummed paper to build the foundations. She promised to show us how to add things like noses. Maybe I'll be able to tell you tomorrow."

Now that her sketch was finished, Ceretha turned on a TV program that held her attention for a long while. Finally, she dropped off to sleep. That was where Mama found her when she returned.

The next day seemed endless. The time was approaching for the first marking period, and the teachers were drilling and reviewing. Ceretha found herself finding fault with her teachers for spending so much time going over material which she already knew. She felt that the children who didn't know by now ought to study at home or stay after school so that the rest of the class wouldn't have to be bored with the same old stuff. If things like reading, spelling, and arithmetic must take up the greater part of the day, keeping her from the excitement of art, then it at least ought to be new reading, spelling, and arithmetic.

"Gracious," she said to Althea in an exasperated tone, when the bell sounded at fifteen after two, "I thought that period would never end. Why on earth does Miss Jones keep going over and over planets and the solar system?"

"Listen, girl, just 'cause you and Marcus and a couple of other kids ketch on real quick, don't think everybody does. When we have that science exam next week, I'm bound to flunk. Never could get that stuff straight. And don't tell me I don't try. I ain't dumb, either, but I jest can't get science."

"I've just been itching to get to Miss Goodwin's class."

"Me, I don't care nothin' about art either. I get along okay, but I'm hoping we get play acting next semester—or even music is better'n art. Lotsa kids is like that. You know what? If Miss Goodwin wasn't so nice, I betcha lotsa kids would raise sand in that room."

111

Things didn't move as quickly in the art class as Ceretha had anticipated. Each child's sketch had to be studied, corrected, and approved before the teacher was ready to begin the actual process. Unfortunately, some of the children did not have their masks sketched yet. Althea was one of these.

When the masks finally were finished, they were to be hung around the room.

"We can't wait forever for the tortoises," said Miss Goodwin. "We'll hang the finished ones this afternoon. Then we'll pick the best three or four."

Miss Goodwin was pleased, and proud of their work. There were masks of almost every description. The boys, for the most part, had tried to see how hideous they could make theirs. Only a few girls experimented with horrid faces; they were more apt to stick to just faces or try to make them very pretty.

Throughout the project, Barbara had been very secretive about her mask. She moved her adjustable table to a corner where she could work with her back to most of her classmates. Miss Goodwin permitted her children a great deal of freedom, because she felt that it contributed to their ability to create. Few children abused the privilege.

Only once during the week did anyone get a look at Bab's work. She had gone to the cupboard for some material she needed. As might be expected, it was Althea who prompted the meddling. She knew enough to keep out of trouble herself, and she also knew which of her fellow classmates needed only an invitation to mischief. She studied the children who were working near Barbara and picked out Hal Meeks as a likely candidate. She was painting her own mask, but in no hurry. She laid her brush down and casually went over to Hal's table.

"Say, Hal," she began quietly, "how come ol' Barbara Smith's gotta cover her mask up every time she goes after somethin'? Her's ain't no better'n nobody else's. I've got a good mind to go over there and snatch that piece of brown paper from over it."

Hal reacted exactly as she had expected.

"Naw!" he whispered. " 'Spose Miss Goodwin sees you. You wanta see it?"

"Yeah! Don't you?"

"Sure! Tell you what, I'll go over there and lift it up real quick, then we can both see it."

Hal moved stealthily to Barbara's desk and raised the brown paper which she used to protect her mask. When he was certain Althea had seen it, he replaced the paper and moved back to his place.

"Pshaw! What's she keepin' that covered up for? 'Taint nothing but a black face."

Althea curled her lip and gestured once with her hands to express utter disgust. Her curiosity had been satisfied, so she went back to her work with renewed zest.

Ceretha had made no attempt to be secretive about her elf's face. The addition of the elongated nose and oversized ears had made it necessary for her to seek Miss Goodwin's aid frequently. She was justly proud of it when it was hung alongside the others.

Miss Goodwin and Barbara were the only ones who were not amazed at Barbara's mask. What Hal and Althea had thought was just another comic black face had turned out to be a superb Nubian head. Wanda Goodwin found it hard to believe that a fifth grader had made it.

The class unanimously agreed that Bab's Nubian was the best of the masks. It was hung where it could be easily seen by people passing the door. This spot was considered the place of honor. There was something noble and elegant about the expression Barbara had captured, and the huge earrings which she had painted in his ears added to the dignity of the drawing.

Babs even smiled at Ceretha that Friday evening as they left the school building. Ceretha met Bernadette at the usual place. Julia joined them, and they started home. Before they left the playground, Ceretha remembered that she had forgotten her rain scarf. When she entered the art class, she had rolled it up tightly and stuck it under her desk.

"Wait for me a minute," she said, "I'll be right back."

Luckily, she met Miss Goodwin at the door nearest to their classroom.

"I left my rain scarf under my desk, Miss Goodwin, may I go and get it?"

"The door is locked, Ceretha, but if you'll hurry, I will let you use my key. Run. I want to get downtown before the stores close."

Ceretha ran as fast as she could and was back in no time with the scarf in her hand. She thanked Miss Goodwin and caught up with Bernadette and Julia.

On Monday morning, Ceretha was as anxious to get to school as she had been the previous week. Two special events were to take place that coming Friday—the Halloween party and the first report cards. She fidgeted so much while Mama was combing her hair that Mama said, "If you're not careful, you will work yourself up to a fever before Friday rolls around."

The day moved along at its usual pace, and in due time, the last period arrived. Ceretha went to art class in great excitement. The moment she entered the door, she realized that things were not right.

Miss Goodwin was not her usual smiling self. When the class was seated and quiet, she said, "I hardly know how to say this, because I still don't want to believe that it is true. All day I have kept telling myself that there is a mistake somewhere and

that the explanation will be forthcoming. If you look at the masks, you will see that Barbara Smith's mask is gone."

The whole class gasped. "Is there anyone in this class," Miss Goodwin went on, "who knows anything about it? It was missing when I came into the room this morning. I have talked with the janitor, and he says it was not here on Friday when he came to empty the wastebaskets. He remembers, because he spent quite sometime looking at the masks. He says there wasn't one of the kind that I described."

No one spoke. The children looked from one to another. Suddenly, Ceretha stood up. "Miss Goodwin, I guess I was the last one in the room on Friday, and I'm sure Barbara's mask was still hanging up. You remember, you let me use your key."

"I do remember. I've remembered little else since I entered this room, and I cannot believe that you would do such an ugly trick."

"But I didn't. The mask was here."

By this time, Babs was crying. Her friends in the room were looking accusingly at Ceretha. Miss Goodwin was struggling within her own mind. She could not believe that Ceretha would stand before the whole class and without flinching admit that she was the last child in the room if she had taken the mask.

117

She asked Ceretha to come out into the hall. They went over the whole situation together. Naturally, Ceretha's story was the same. The teacher then asked her if she was sure she had locked the door. Ceretha was almost positive that she had, though she did not recall checking it as she left. When they went back into the room, Miss Goodwin said she did not believe that Ceretha had taken the mask, but she had no idea what could have happened to it.

That night Brown Rabbit told Mama and Papa what had happened and repeated it for Ruth Ann later on. "Miss Goodwin believes me, but lots of the children don't and that's no fun."

10

The three days preceding the Halloween party turned out to be anything but exciting and enjoyable. Barbara's mask failed to show up, and the class was no closer to solving the mystery of its disappearance on Thursday than they had been on Monday. Miss Goodwin helped Babs make a new one, but it lacked the inspiration which had made the first one so special.

Ceretha, along with the rest of the class, had gone on with designing a costume for the party. The fact that many of her classmates persisted in their belief that she had destroyed Barbara's mask made her unhappy. She also found it hard to concentrate when she was in other classes. In the art class, she worked mechanically, taking no real interest in what she was doing.

Miss Goodwin spoke to her about her lack of enthusiasm.

"You know, Ceretha, I am disappointed in your costume design."

"Why, Miss Goodwin?"

"Let's get at the answer to that by having you answer some questions for me. First, are you satisfied with it?"

"Well, I—"

"I didn't think you were. What's wrong with it?"

"I'm not sure. Some places I wasn't very careful with the paints; it's messy in spots."

Miss Goodwin put her arm around Ceretha and said, "All true, but the real reason is your heart wasn't in it."

Ceretha made no attempt to answer, instead she put her brush down and idly fingered the edge of the table. Her eyes were full of tears. The teacher went on, "I've watched you since Monday. Your work hasn't been the same. I know you did not take Barbara's mask. I'm still hoping that we'll find out what really happened to it."

"But the children—" Ceretha managed to say before the tears spilled over.

"That's the hardest part, isn't it? Let's keep hoping. You may take your design home today."

Miss Goodwin moved on to another child's desk. It was some time before Ceretha could completely regain her composure. One or two of the children near her had noticed the tears, but fortunately they were her friends. That made it easier to bear.

Babs had grown more and more spiteful each day. She had, of course, repeated the story to Marlene and Celestine, even though Miss Goodwin had asked the class to promise to keep it a class secret. That afternoon as Ceretha, Bernadette, and Julia were walking home, Barbara and Marlene passed them. Marlene went out of her way to brush against Ceretha, and hiss, "Sneak-thief!"

"I am no such thing!"

"Push her back, Ceretha," Bernadette urged. "You ain't done nothing to her."

"Let's not have a fight, Bernadette. Come on, Ceretha," Julia quaked.

"I don't want to fight, but I'm not exactly nonviolent, if people pick on me without a good reason," Ceretha stated flatly.

Barbara intervened with, "Marlene, I'll thank you to let me handle my own affairs."

Julia took Ceretha by the hand, and the three girls walked on. Every so often, Julia or Bernadette would try to start a conversation, but it would immediately go flat. When they reached Julia's house, Ceretha did manage, "See you in the morning." At her own door, Ceretha asked, listlessly, "Coming in, Bernadette?"

Bernadette hesitated a minute, then said, "Naw! I don't reckon you feel like being bothered."

Another time Ceretha would have protested, but this time she just muttered, "See you, then."

Bernadette stood on the steps several minutes after Ceretha had gone inside. When she finally realized that there was nothing she could do to help her friend, she went slowly up the steps. She was not satisfied though as she was not certain she had explored every means of help. On each step she racked her brain for an idea. At the door of their apartment she put her hand to her neck to get the door key, which she always wore on a string. Instead of the key, she pulled out her religious medal. She dropped it as if it had burned her; found the key, dashed into her bedroom, tied a scarf on her head and ran down the steps again.

"I shoulda done it at first," she said, as she jumped the last four steps.

No one who saw Bernadette as she raced up the street would have suspected that she was on her way to church. When she passed the settlement-house playground, several children called to her, but she only waved. She didn't slow down when she reached the church, either. Father Paul was on his way out the door, and Bernadette ran smack into him.

"Someone ill, Bernadette?" he asked.

"No, Father," she said, "please 'scuse me. I jes' gotta pray in a hurry for a friend."

Father Paul made no attempt to detain her further. He decided that any friend of Bernadette's who needed praying for that urgently, might benefit by his added prayer that evening.

As Ceretha told Mama about the talk with Miss Goodwin and showed her the completed sketch of the costume, she did not know that Bernadette was reverently genuflecting and praying at each Station of the Cross in St. Agnes Church.

"I guess I should have asked Bernadette to come in, Mama," she said, "she seemed sort of disappointed, but I just don't feel like talking."

"It's much better that you talk though, dear. Brooding doesn't really help the situation any."

"Nothing's helping this situation. I told you, didn't I, that Miss Goodwin said she was not satisfied with my design."

"Perhaps we can remedy that in the dyeing and making of the costume. I have some unbleached muslin that has been washed and shrunk. I can tie dye it so that it will make a very pretty Jack Frost suit."

"Okay!" was all Ceretha answered.

Mama suggested that since they were eating alone that they do so right away and then they would have more time to work on the costume. Ceretha played with the food on her plate, eating very little. Papa had told Mama early that morning that perhaps if she planned an extra special dinner with several of Brown Rabbit's favorites she'd forget the unhappiness at school.

When Mama began to clear the table for dessert, she said, "Wait until you see what we have for dessert."

Ceretha just looked at Mama without saying a word. She decided to try to eat the treat, but everything stuck in her throat. Mama put a generous piece of ginger cake before her and along with it a pitcher of rich, old-fashioned vanilla sauce. This was truly one of Ceretha's favorites. Mama thought she was dreadfully slow pouring the sauce, but she didn't say anything. Finally, she began to eat.

"It's good, Mama," but that was as far as she got. That stuck in her throat, too, and the tears began to trickle down. She left the table, and went to her room. Mama made no effort to follow her. She felt it was best to let her cry it out.

Mama was right; Ceretha was back before the dishes were finished. She picked up a towel and helped with the drying and putting away before either of them talked again. Then she said, "If Barbara knew me better, she'd know that I wouldn't have taken her mask for anything."

"Then, the thing for you to do, dear, is to try to see that she gets to know you better."

"But I've tried, Mama, ever so hard."

"Remember what your Papa says, 'If at first you don't succeed, try, try again.' Shall we get to your costume now?"

After considerable discussion, they decided it would be best to dye the material in three small sections, rather than to try to tie and dye the whole three or four yards of cloth. Mama had bought a vivid green for the basic color; crimson, yellow and brown for the other splashes of color. Ceretha's spirits did brighten some when she saw the first piece dyed for the jacket. The pants were to be cut from the second piece, and the pointed-toed shoes and the Robin-Hood hat from the third.

When they had hung the last section to dry, Ceretha found a heavy piece of cardboard from which she made herself an artist's palette. She tried the dye solution for the spots of paint, but the paper absorbed the color. She set it to dry and said she would color it with crayon the next evening. Mama was going to make the suit the next day so that it would be ready for fitting when Brown Rabbit came home from school. At bedtime, Mama was sure Ceretha was on the road to recovery.

By Thursday afternoon, the spirit of Halloween was very much alive again in class fifty-four, in

125

spite of the mysterious disappearance of Barbara's mask. There were so many last minute things to be done that nobody in the class had time to be ugly to anyone else. The adjustable worktables had to be folded and stacked in the least conspicuous place. The boys had left pumpkins that were to be made into jack-o-lanterns for a last minute job. Then there was the job of cleaning off Miss Goodwin's desk. She often said it had a way of getting cluttered up like no other teacher's. She assigned this task to Barbara and Ceretha, thinking that perhaps it might bring the two a little closer together. Ceretha, of course, was willing; Barbara took the job rather reluctantly, and Miss Goodwin pretended not to notice.

"If you'll move the books from that side while I get these off this side, we'll get through quicker," Ceretha said.

Barbara moved the books without answering. As she did, Ceretha noticed that a piece of paper fell to the floor. She put down her books and bent to pick up the paper. Across the folded sheet was scrawled in red marking pencil, "Attention! Miss Wanda Goodwin."

Ceretha thought she'd best ask if it was something Miss Goodwin wanted before she threw it in the wastebasket.

"Where did that come from?" Miss Goodwin asked.

"Off your desk, when Barbara moved some books," Ceretha replied.

"I don't recall any message addressed to me in red pencil."

Ceretha went back to her cleaning. Miss Goodwin leaned against the cupboard and read the note. If any of the children had been watching her, they would have noticed the smile which spread across her face. She began clapping her hands to attract the class's attention, and at the same time calling, "Children, children, listen to this."

She was waving the paper in the air. It took a few moments for the class to come to order. Then Miss Goodwin began to read. "Wait," she said, "the first paragraph won't interest you. Here's the place.

"I saw the beautiful Nubian mask through the door, and since you weren't here to give me permission to borrow it, I used my passkey, leaving you this note in its place.

Thanks.

Letitia B. Lenier

P. S. *Send one of your children for it whenever you are ready. I'd like for my high school classes to see it."*

"Do you know who Mrs. Lenier is? I owe you an apology, especially Ceretha."

Most of the children knew that Mrs. Lenier was the head of the high school art department. It seemed that she had been trying to catch Miss Goodwin on the day that the mask disappeared to borrow some of the things that her children had made. Mrs. Lenier wanted to show them at a lecture she was giving at the Y.W.C.A. When she reached the room after school, Miss Goodwin was gone, and Mrs. Lenier left the note which had slipped down between some books on the desk.

There was great rejoicing in the room from then on. In fact, they had to spend some time after the close of school to complete the tasks they had begun.

Miss Goodwin sent Barbara to retrieve her mask. Everybody went home that afternoon hardly able to wait for the next day.

Ceretha had only one cloud in her sky, as she rushed out of the school building to tell Bernadette and Julia the good news. When Bernadette saw her friend smiling, she began to smile, knowingly. "They foun' that false face, didn't they?" she asked.

"Yes," Ceretha replied.

"How did you know, Bernadette?" Julia exclaimed. "They just found it last period."

"I knowed they's going to fin' it today, though. I went to church yestiddy evenin' and prayed fuh you."

"Oh, thank you Bernadette."

Mama's eyes glistened strangely when Ceretha told her about Bernadette going to the church to pray. Ruth Ann was there, but she didn't say anything. Mama said, "Bless the child."

The Friday of the Halloween party was one of the happiest days of the school year for Ceretha. They received their report cards in their homeroom that morning. Ceretha had made straight A's. The only A student in her class. Marcus had a B in science and Babs had two—one in science and one in social studies.

Miss Goodwin said she just had to meet Ceretha's Mama when she saw the Jack Frost suit.

11

With the clearing up of the "mask mystery," life once more became wonderful for Ceretha. Everyone at school and settlement house was busy with Thanksgiving plans.

Nat's combined dancing classes were having a program showing various kinds of dances used to celebrate harvest feasts around the world. The square dance groups were presenting dances from the American pioneer period. Ceretha's favorites were two that were done to the music of "Turkey-in-the-Straw" and "Jingle Bells."

Ceretha had picked up some of the steps when

the three groups met for joint rehearsals. Bernadette's dancing had not improved greatly, but she made an excellent caller. She was too bashful to say that she liked calling for the dances, so Ceretha had to tell Nat. Natascha was delighted, and she helped Bernadette to improve her technique.

One evening when Papa came home from work, he opened the kitchen door and called out, "What's going on in here? Sounds like barn dance night."

"The children are getting ready for the Wickham House Festival. Bernadette is going to be the caller," said Mama.

"I used to cut quite a figure, Rosie. Believe I'll watch for a while. Supper's not ready, anyway, is it?"

"No, Harvey. And I shan't rush if you're going in to join the children."

"I'm just going to watch."

Mama nodded her head knowingly. She watched Papa fling his coat and hat on a kitchen chair, instead of taking them into the bedroom. He fairly skipped when he went into the living room.

Harvey must be getting more used to his work, Mama thought. He seems less fagged out these days.

Papa stood in the doorway for sometime before the girls saw him. When Brown Rabbit did see him she cried, "Papa! Oh, we're having the most fun. Listen how Bernadette calls the dances."

"Go on with your dance. Reminds me of my youth. I used to cut a pretty fine step m'self."

"Come dance with me now, we need another person, Papa. Bernadette is the caller and isn't dancing."

"Aw, child, now what would an old man like me look like traipsin' over the floor?"

Mama was listening from the kitchen. She made a private wager that it wouldn't be two minutes before Papa would be joining the dance.

Ceretha kept egging him on. "The girls want to see you dance. Come on, Papa."

"Well," Papa said. rising slowly, "just this once now. I'm too old for this kind of foolishness."

"Call 'Turkey in the Straw' again, Bernadette. Now make believe there are two other couples in this square. Here we go now."

For at least half an hour nothing could be heard in the Brown apartment but, "Swing your partner, promenade all, do-si-do, left hands all, balance right, a left-hand grand" mingled with the shuffling of feet. The people in the tailor shop must have wondered what could be going on; they'd never heard that much noise out of the Browns in the eight and one-half weeks they had been there.

The "Fireman's Dance" and "Jingle Bells" followed the "Turkey in the Straw" before Papa, out of breath, called a halt.

"Whoa! Whoa!" he said. "I'm an old man, children." He literally collapsed on the sofa. Mama had been watching in the doorway, enjoying the performance.

"You still cut a pretty caper, Harve," she said.

"But my wind's so short." Papa panted.

Time goes by quickly when people are enjoying themselves. When Papa sat down, Bernadette glanced out of the window and exclaimed, "My goodness, but it's dark outside already. I betta be gettin' upstairs. Is it six o'clock yet, Mister Brown?"

"It must be, child. I left the mill at four-thirty. Why, it is already a quarter past six."

"Mother Dear may be home. I'm going to ketch the dickens. I washed up the brea'fus dishes, but I didn't make up my bed. I was in such a hurry to get down here and practice them dances."

"I have to go, too, Ceretha," Julia said. "May I call my house? My brother's coming to walk Sharon and me home." Julia moved toward the telephone. When she came back, she announced, "Sharon, Johnny says we should meet him out front. He wants to get back in time for a TV program."

The group in the Browns's living room heard Julia and Sharon speak to someone as they passed through the areaway. Bernadette, followed by Mama, moved quickly to the kitchen.

"If that is your mother, Bernadette, ask her to

134

come in for a while, won't you? Seems we never find time to just visit."

Bernadette opened the door and called, "Mother Dear, that you?" Mrs. Hughes's high, strident voice reflected the physical and mental strain she was undergoing daily.

"How come you cain't never stay home no mo'? Effen you ain't at the Wickham House, you's at Mis Brown's."

Ceretha's mother made her way to the door. "Good evening, Mrs. Hughes. I realize you are tired and probably have things to do at home, but won't you come in for a little while?"

Marie Hughes was not too much taller or heavier than her gangly daughter. She wore an ill-fitting, dark green coat. It looked as if it was turning brown at the seams and in several other spots where it had constantly been creased. On her head was a small, green hat. She held a small bag of groceries in one arm and clutched a well-worn, black patent-leather purse under the other arm.

She stood outside the Browns' door. She was rather hesitant about coming in, even though she had been invited. There was something about the cheery cleanliness of Mrs. Brown's kitchen that made it all the harder to bear her own shabby, half-cleaned apartment.

Mama kept holding the door open, so Mrs.

Hughes succumbed and came in. Ceretha watched from the doorway between the kitchen and living room. Mama offered Mrs. Hughes a chair, and as she did so, she was thinking how prematurely old and tired Mrs. Hughes looked.

"I won't keep you long," she said. "Really I am ashamed of myself. I've been intending for weeks to come upstairs and pay you a real visit."

Mrs. Hughes winced. Mama went on, "Our children are such good friends we ought to know each other better. It would never have been this way back home."

"No'm," Mrs. Hughes murmured. "Sometimes I wishes we'd neva' come up here. We ain't that much better off."

"I know exactly how you feel. We pulled up our roots too, sold our home, left all our friends, and came here because we—that is Ruth Ann, our eldest daughter—felt it would be better for Ceretha. I've had some bad days in these past months, too. Harve, my husband says, we've just got to have faith and things will be better."

"That's what my Joe, he keep sayin'. We come here with nothin', and 'pears like we going stay that way. That's how I feel. I works and he works and it don't look like we gettin' nowhere."

"Takes time," Mama answered. "I wanted to talk to you about Bernadette."

"She been bad?"

"Goodness no!" Mama put her arm around Bernadette. "She's a good child, a very good child. She's always welcome here. Of course, it really isn't my business, but don't you think ten is rather young to expect her to stay upstairs alone, especially through the winter months?"

"Yes'um. I use to let huh go to Wickham House eva evenin', but Bernadette ain't got no remembrance when it comes time to quit playin'. Eva evenin' she be late comin' home. Now I lets huh go after supper and stay tell nine o'clock. She say you won't let your lil' girl go eva evenin'. It's a nice place for them to play."

"I know, but I don't approve of children being out of the home every night. Ceretha goes to the Book Club meeting on Tuesday evening from five-thirty until seven o'clock and to the Saturday morning dancing class."

"Yes'um, but I cain't stand to hear Bernadette's mouf eva evenin', all evenin'. Sometimes I'm so tired I cain't stand myself. You all don't know how much I 'preciate you all lettin' Bernadette come down here. When she home she don't do nuthin' but talk about the nice things you all got and Ceretha's pretty clothes. I been intendin' to fix up our place eva since we come here, but I be's so tired I don't do nuthin' but fix a lil' somethin' to eat and straighten 'round."

"It must be awfully hard to work all day and

have to come home and keep house. I haven't experienced that yet. Why don't you give Bernadette permission to stay here each evening until you get home? She isn't one bit of trouble, and besides, she'll be company for Ceretha."

"Yes'um she kin stay. Thank you so much."

Before Mama could answer, their back door opened and Ruth Ann came in. Ceretha thought she felt an icy chill in the room as Ruth gave Mrs. Hughes a very cold "Good evening!"

The Hugheses left as quickly as possible, after Bernadette's mother had mumbled a return greeting.

Mama had asked Ruthie to supper as Bertram was working the four to twelve shift. Ruth Ann began apologizing for being late.

"I was certain that I was holding you up, Mama, but I am going to a bridge party tomorrow evening, and I didn't have a single blouse to wear with my new suit. I rushed downtown from work thinking that I'd surely make it home by six-thirty. I'll show you the blouse after supper. Bert's going to scold when he finds out about it. He thinks I am extravagant about clothes."

Papa, who was getting very hungry, came and stood beside Ceretha.

"Bert's probably right, Ruth Ann. Don't believe I've seen you twice in the same get-up since we came here. Vanity is a sin, child."

"Oh, Papa, I'm not that bad."

"Help your Mama get the supper on the table. I'm nearly starved. Women spend too much time prettin' themselves up these days instead of looking after their husbands."

Papa said the blessing, and then leaned back and looked fondly at his two daughters. "Look at them, Rosie! Ruthie grown and married, and it won't be too many years before we'll be losing the Rabbit."

"But, Papa," Brown Rabbit interrupted, "don't you remember I promised to wait until I meet a man just like you, and Mama says they don't make them any more!"

"True, true! At least he'll be hard to find, if you'll pardon my saying so. You'll mean to wait, baby, but some man'll come along and sweep you off your feet like Bert did Ruthie. Which reminds me, Ruth Ann, you and Bert been married going on three years now, and I've been expecting a grandchild!"

Ruth colored, "Oh, Papa!"

"I'm serious," Papa went on, "don't you and Bert want children?"

"Yes, Papa, when we can afford them."

"Poppycock! You are a lot better off financially than Rosie and I were when you came."

"It was different then, Papa. When Bert and I have a home and have saved a little money, then we'll think about children; certainly not while we are living here."

"What's the world coming to? In our day we just praised God for sending children."

"Living's harder in the city, Harve," Mama said. "And young people today don't think as you and I did. Don't worry, you'll be a grandpapa yet."

The rest of the meal was eaten in comparative silence. Mama and Ruth talked a bit about the coming bridge party. Ruthie said she was to have her club next month, and she hated the thought of having them come into this neighborhood. Papa opened his mouth as if he was going to say something, then snapped it closed. Ceretha was glad because Papa and Ruthie sometimes had terrible arguments, and Papa blamed it on Ruth Ann's association with uppity people.

Why Mama ever brought up the subject of Bernadette and her mother, Ceretha could not figure out, but Mama did.

"I feel so sorry for that poor Mrs. Hughes. She seemed so downtrodden."

"She's just shiftless," Ruth Ann stated flatly.

"I don't agree with you, Ruthie."

"Look at her; look at that child, Mama. I'll bet you'd have to shovel your way into that apartment. I cringe every time I see Ceretha with her."

That was when Papa put his paper down. Papa was angry. Ceretha was watching him; Ruth Ann was not. She went on. "Ceretha will never be able to make friends with children who are anybody as

140

long as she persists in taking that awful-looking creature with her."

"Bernadette's not homely, Ruth Ann. Have you ever really studied her face?" Mama asked.

That's when Papa exploded, "Of course she hasn't. Ruth Ann sees nothing beyond fine clothes, big houses, and fancy automobiles. Even her religion's got to be fancied up. If I thought that Brown Rabbit would grow up a bigoted, vain young woman because of increased advantages, I'd pack up and go right back to New Hope tomorrow."

Ruth Ann had some strong feelings on the subject, also. "Papa, I'm sorry you feel that way, but this is not New Hope, Mississippi, and standards here are different. It is important to be accepted, and people just aren't accepting folk like the Hugheses with open arms."

Papa growled out, "Fiddlesticks!" Then he stalked out of the room.

There was dead silence for a few seconds after Papa left. Ceretha broke the silence with, "Ruthie, Bernadette's MY friend no matter who likes her or doesn't like her."

12

Ceretha was slower than usual getting bathed and dressed the morning after the heated discussion about the Hughes family. The quarrel between Ruth Ann and Papa, and the hurt over her sister's inability to accept her best friend were uppermost in Ceretha's thoughts when she awakened. She could hear Mama moving about in the kitchen, and she knew that if she did not appear shortly, Mama would call out to her to hurry. Sometimes it was very irritating to have adults tell you to do the thing you were on the very verge of doing. She wanted to get to the kitchen before Mama called, because she did not need another thing to add to her present discomfort. She slid into her place at the breakfast table before Mama had to call her.

"My goodness you're a sour-puss this morning," Mama remarked, "I hope you aren't still fretting about last night. Ruth Ann has already been down here. She and Papa are the best of friends once more."

"I'm glad they made up, Mama, but what really bothers me most, I guess—is the way Ruthie looks at Bernadette. I'm so uncomfortable when they're in the same room. I want to take Bernadette by the hand and run away. Do you understand how I feel, Mama?"

"Yes, I do understand, Ceretha, but I'm not giving up hope."

Ceretha picked up her glass of juice, sipped in silence, then pushed it aside. "I don't know if it's me or the juice. It doesn't taste right; everything's wrong this morning. Even my knee hurts."

"You've said something about your knee hurting before. Which knee? Come around here and let me have a look at it."

Reluctantly, Ceretha submitted to Mama's examination of her right knee. She winced a little when Mama pressed very hard. Mama's fingers were deft and gentle as she probed. "It's a little swollen. I've read that it's best to have things like this checked immediately, especially with growing children, Brown Rabbit."

"Oh! Mama," Ceretha exploded, "It's nothing. I probably hit it against my bed, or something."

"Nevertheless, we're going to have it looked after. Now, let me see if I can find the doctor's name and telephone number Ruth Ann gave me. I tucked it away somewhere. I'll just call her before she leaves for work and write it in the proper place." When she returned, she said, "Ruth Ann agrees with me. Even if it is nothing, a doctor ought to have a look at it."

"Okay, if it's still hurting this afternoon, we can go right after school."

"No, we ought not take a chance on its getting worse. You can afford to miss one day of school."

Ceretha's rebuttal was interrupted by the appearance of Bernadette, "You're not ready for school yet? What's the matter?"

"My big mouth, mostly. I told Mama about my knee, and—"

"And we're going to have a doctor see it this morning," Mama completed Ceretha's sentence. "You'd better hurry now, Bernadette. We'll see you after school."

Ceretha checked Bernadette's departure with, "Tell Julia to call me as soon as she gets home. We gotta go to the library for some stuff on tribal dances."

"I'll tell her eff I see her. She ain't liable to be ready." Bernadette turned again to leave. Before she could open the door, it was opened by Ruth Ann. Mama noticed that Bernadette greeted Ruth, with what for her, was unusual charm, and while Ruth Ann's response was not the warmest, it was not her customary, cold "How do you do?"

Ruth took one look at Ceretha and said, "You certainly are not your usual bright and cheery self this morning, little sister."

"I don't feel bright and cheery, and I don't see why you and Mama—" She did not get to finish the sentence. Mama said, in no uncertain terms, that she was about at the end of her patience. Ruth pecked Ceretha on the cheek, and suggested that she lie down again. Mama asked Ruth Ann to have a cup of coffee, and the two of them sat down to talk.

"If you get to the doctor's office early, Mama— that is a little before eleven—and if you are lucky, maybe Ceretha can go on to school after lunch. I'll call Dr. Barnes's office as soon as I get to work. This is just one of the things that used to worry me when you were in New Hope, thirty miles from the nearest doctor. And I never liked Dr. Marble." She drew on her snow-white gloves with a kind of proficient air which seemed to indicate that she had

145

the situation well in hand. She kissed her mother firmly on the cheek and left. Moments later the door opened again; Ruth Ann moved quickly across the room to where her mother was standing. She stuck her hand into Mama's apron pocket and headed back out of the door, "Just taxi fare, Mama."

By ten-thirty, Ceretha's mood had improved some. She and Mama waited in the door of the tailor shop for the cab. They reminisced about old Doctor Marble who had come to the college once a month to check on the health of students. He gave inoculations against malaria and typhoid at the beginning of each school year, TB tests somewhat later, and if in between times, someone became ill, he was transported the thirty miles from New Hope to Ashton. The Browns had gone to Ashton to the dentist and to shop. About twice a year, Papa'd suggest that they see Dr. Marble. "Better let him thump us all on the chest and tell us that we're all right."

Ceretha had always enjoyed these visits. Dr. Marble's office and home were combined, and his hobby was breeding cocker spaniels. If one of the dogs had had a new litter, and if Mama and Papa were not in a hurry, Dr. Marble would take Ceretha back to the kennels to play with the puppies. The family had gone to see Dr. Marble just a day or two before they left New Hope for good. Dr. Marble had walked out to the car with them that day.

"Hate to see you all go, Harvey," he'd told Papa. "Never believed you could solve anythin' by runnin' away from it. If all the forthright and educated Nigras keep leaving the South, we'll never lick this thing. But, a man has to do what he has to do. Tell Ruth Ann I thought I was goin' to have the pleasure of deliverin' your first grandbaby." Dr. Marble had taken Papa's hand with both of his hands to say good-bye.

Dr. Barnes's office was nothing like Dr. Marble's. It was in a large office building in a shopping center. The air-conditioned, dimly lighted waiting room was a far cry from the homey, chintz curtained room in Ashton. Soft music was coming from a public address system when they entered. There were several people in the room ahead of Ceretha and Mama. Shortly after their arrival, a young woman in a white uniform came into the room and asked if there was a Mrs. Harvey Brown there. When Mama identified herself, the young woman came over and said, "I'm Constance Cook. Ruth Ann called and said that you would be in." She put her hand on Ceretha's shoulder. "We can get your history, if you and your mother'll come this way."

"Hadn't we better wait?" Mama asked. "There are others ahead of us."

Constance Cook gave a quick glance around the room. "They're all old friends, Mrs. Brown. Doctor isn't in, and we can save time by taking this information for him. I don't know if Ruth Ann told you, but we belong to the same bridge club."

Mrs. Cook went on, "Dr. Barnes shouldn't be long in coming. He's making rounds at the hospital, but he's not scheduled for surgery today." She guided Mama and Ceretha into a small office. Mama had to answer what seemed to Ceretha like millions of questions that had nothing to do with her knee. Finally, Mrs. Cook took Ceretha's temperature, gave her a blue card to hold, and said that they might return to the waiting room.

Ceretha had been having fun trying to figure out what Dr. Barnes was going to look like—envisioning him as a brown version of Dr. Marble. She was all wrong, Dr. Barnes was nothing like Dr. Marble. He was much, much younger. He was short, very dark, and sported a goatee. Ceretha was not at all certain that she liked his crisp, detached manner. He asked Mama questions which were not on the printed form and emitted grunting sounds as he proceeded with the examination. After sometime, he spoke directly to Ceretha, "Young lady, I'm not certain what we have here. May not be serious, in fact probably isn't, but we'd like to be sure. We want you to go to the hospital for some tests and X rays."

"Hospital?" Mama and Ceretha asked together.

Dr. Barnes turned toward the intercom and said, "Hospital! We'd like for you to take the young lady to St. Luke's, Mrs. Brown, unless you have some serious objection." He didn't give Mama time to answer. "You won't need an appointment, but get there early. Someone at the hospital will direct you. We should have the results back in a day or so after the pictures are made. In the meantime, we want you to stay off the leg, Ceretha—not necessarily in bed. Keep it elevated as much as possible. If there should be pain, give her an aspirin and put an ice bag to the knee. One of the girls in the office will contact you when we're ready." He stood up as if they were dismissed.

Mama asked about the fees. "Mrs. Cook will tell you about that on your way out. She will have Ceretha's card by the time you get to her desk." Ceretha was sure now that she didn't like him; he wasn't even courteous.

After she paid the bill, Mama inquired as to the best way to get a taxi back home. Mrs. Cook said that she would call one for them, and that they should wait at the north entrance of the building. "I'll give them your description, Mrs. Brown, so that the cabbie won't get the wrong fare. It's been nice meeting both of you and don't worry about Ceretha's knee. Dr. Barnes is a very thorough man."

Ceretha grumbled in the cab about the unnecessary time she was missing from school. She knew what Dr. Marble would have been able to recognize a "silly old bump on the knee" for what it was, and there would have been no need for staying out of school. Mama, too, was a little perturbed by Dr. Barnes.

That evening Ruth Ann assured them that Dr. Barnes was not only competent but also interested, "He wanted me to reassure you that the X rays are a routine check to confirm his diagnosis."

"What diagnosis?" Papa wanted to know. "From what your Mama has told me that man didn't say what was ailing her leg."

"That's just the point, Papa. He isn't going to say anything until he is absolutely sure." Then Ruth Ann deliberately changed the subject, "Bert's working a double. He called this afternoon, too. I thought I'd eat supper with you folk, if it's all right. I have a club meeting at eight, and I can go up and change clothes after I help with the dishes."

"Since when do you have to ask if it's all right to sit at our table, Madam? Your Mama looks like she's even more pleased than I. I've been wondering about Bert and all these doubles. That boy's driving himself too hard."

"I know, Papa," Ruth went on, "I keep telling him that, but he's determined that we get out of this neighborhood as soon as possible. He says he can't afford to turn down a double right now, because his boss promised him a straight day shift after Christmas. If he doesn't get back into school soon, his G.I. Bill help will run out. He needs a little more than a year to get his degree."

"I share his feelings about the neighborhood, but I don't, for the life of me, see that much difference between segregation in the South and here, Ruth Ann."

"Now, Papa—"

"Don't now, Papa, me. Every place that Bert has looked at houses the neighborhood's either all colored or turnin' fast. Take those folk moving from Woodside; all they're doing is building a high class ghetto on the other side of town."

Mama intervened, "Don't let your Papa get all steamed up about the race problem, Ruth Ann. The only place he can bestir himself to, other than church and work, since we've been here is an NAACP meeting. Harvey, you know you are neglecting your youngest daughter, and she's not in the best of humor. Why don't you go in the living room and cheer her up while Ruth Ann helps me get the supper on."

They ended up with Papa and Ceretha having their supper on snack trays in front of the television.

Before Ruth Ann left for her club meeting, she reassured them that Dr. Barnes would not delay the report on Ceretha's X ray any longer than necessary. Mama, Papa, and Ceretha settled down to television. Papa drifted off to sleep before the third commercial. Mama spent a great deal of the time watching Ceretha. Finally she told herself that she saw no signs of pain, so she relaxed and began to enjoy the movie.

151

The next two days just dragged by for Ceretha. Her leg did not hurt unless she put undue pressure on it. Mama vowed that Ceretha was like a skittish pony. She was bad tempered with everyone. Bernadette, Julia, and Sharon came every day. Julia came by after school one day loaded down with books from the library, including the material on tribal dances. "Girl," she said, "you'd better believe I wouldn't be lugging this many books for just anybody."

"And I'm not just anybody," Ceretha responded. "Today I feel like a mean, old witch, crouched in her cave, just waiting to jump out on unsuspecting little children."

"I can go home, you know."

"Please don't go, Julia. Mama's making gingerbread, and I promise I won't make like a witch, but all these grown-ups, including Dr. Barnes, are making a big thing out of nothing."

"Girl, you ought to have a doctor like mine. My mother just calls him up and tells him how I feel. He calls the drugstore, and they send out some medicine and that's it."

"Tell your mother to tell my Mama about your doctor. Let's see the books you brought. This stuff on Indian dances is wasted on me. Lotta dancing I can do with my leg stuck up in the air."

"Why'd you tell me to bring 'em then?"

"Wishing, I guess. What's going on at school?"

"Oh! Barbara Smith sent you a message."

"Barbara sent me a —"

"Is it your leg or your ear that's stoved up? She said that since you're absent, Mrs. Hudson told her to take over the Social Studies Committee project."

"She would! With seven other people in that group, she'd have to ask Barbara."

"I don't get it, Ceretha. What's with you and this Barbara chick? She's not so special in my book."

"It's not that she's special, Julia."

"Forget her then!"

"It's not that simple. I'm not sure I can make you understand exactly how I feel."

"Well, you've got until six o'clock to try. Johnny's coming for me at six."

"It's not that complicated, either. Barbara and I live in the same block."

"So do—ah—maybe a hundred other kids."

"Are you going to listen, or are you going to tell me?"

"Okay, I'm listening, I'm listening—get on with it."

"She's one of the first people I met when I came here. I've found out that we like a lot of the same things. And most important of all, I guess, she's got the wrong idea about me."

"I still say forget her. How about a game of Scrabble?"

153

13

Papa assessed Ceretha's return visit to Dr. Barnes, and his referral of the case to Dr. G. W. Holmes, an orthopedic specialist, as part of a mammoth conspiracy to keep poor people poor. As it turned out, Ceretha had a collection of fluid in the knee area, from a bump or a sprain. Dr. Holmes admitted that he could have withdrawn the fluid in his own office, but he sent Ceretha to the hospital, because "while we don't expect complications, we prefer cutting down the risks."

Ceretha was home again, shortly after noon of

the day of the "operation." Papa was steaming, "Now, Rosie," he said, "I don't want Brown Rabbit hurt, nor hurting, but it seems to me this has been much ado about nothing."

"And I agree, Papa," Ceretha chimed in. "Dr. Holmes says I'll be good as new in a week. A whole week, mind you."

"Harvey," Mama said quietly, "one crosspatch is all I can stand at a time. Since you don't have to go back to work until tomorrow at midnight, make the best of it. Your insurance from the job will take care of the biggest portion of the bill, and we'll just have to believe that the doctor was doing what he thought was best."

Papa snorted, but he did not argue the point. A little later, he announced that he was going to spend the rest of the day downtown. There was nothing on TV that Ceretha cared to watch. She spent the early afternoon watching the clock, waiting for school to be out. She cautioned Mama to watch out for Bernadette. "She might think I'm still in that silly old hospital."

Bernadette was later than usual coming home, but when she came she was not alone. Ceretha could hear her talking to someone as she came through the gangway. It turned out to be Stuffy. "Hullo, Mrs. Brown," he said, "Babs told us Ceretha was in the hospital, and m'gram sent these brownies for you to take to her. She says she ain't forgot her promise to come and visit. She's going to surprise you real soon."

Mama told them Ceretha was home. She was about to invite Bernadette and Stuffy to go in the living room, when she realized that she was alone. Bernadette had sprinted across the kitchen, and Stuffy was right behind her.

"Lordy, girl," Bernadette shrieked. "Here I was worrying about you and you're settin' up at home. Now ain't that somethin'?"

"Ain't it, though!" Ceretha repeated playfully. "And Stuffy! How about this?"

"You got a cast?" Stuffy quizzed.

"No, it's just bandaged."

"Heck! I was going to give you m' autograph."

The three children laughed loudly at Stuffy's wit. Mama came in carrying a tray with glasses, a pitcher of milk, and some of the brownies Stuffy had brought. As he reached for the last of the cookies, Stuffy snickered, "Boy, my gram would shoot me if she knew I'd come up here and eaten all your brownies, Ceretha. Maybe I can talk her into makin' another batch. Just between us three, I've kind of got a way with Gram, though she declares a hundred times a day that I'm going to drive her to drink or somethin'. Babs gets mad, 'cause she says that Gram is partial to me."

"What's that?" Bernadette asked.

"Likes him best," Ceretha replied. "Stuffy, how'd Barbara happen to mention me and the hospital."

"Just talkin' to Gram. You know how you girls blab. Why?"

"I just wanted to know."

"That makes a lotta sense. Girls are stupid! Take Barbara—she don't play with nobody in this block but Marlene. If Marlene's gone some place, she just sits in the house looking like the world is coming to an end or somethin'. Me, I'm friends with a lotta guys."

"We're not stupid, Stuffy, just different. What's your telephone number?"

"Eight, four, seven, one, nine, three, five, why?"

"I was just thinking that I'd like to call your grandmother and thank her for the brownies. Is Barbara at home?"

"Yeah! Marlene's spending the night with some girl on the north side, so Babs is probably layin' across her bed readin' a book. Guess I better be goin'. It's getting near suppertime, and I'm hungry."

"Hungry?" Bernadette and Ceretha repeated.

"Yeah! Nothing so strange about that," Stuffy commented as he left the room. "See ya," and he was gone.

Between the constant ringing of the telephone and Bernadette's chatter, the time went by very quickly. "Jus' about evabody in your class musta called up here this evenin'."

"Funny thing," Ceretha replied, "I didn't know that many kids in my class would even miss me."

Ruth Ann and Papa came in together. Ruth had a new *Alice's Adventures In Wonderland* for Ceretha. The old copy had been read and reread until it was practically in shreds. Ruth Ann said she had never liked the story until she started reading it to Ceretha, who loved every minute of it.

"Thanks for bringing it, Ruthie," Ceretha said, "but half the fun of *Alice* is hearing it read out loud. If Bernadette can stay a little longer, would you read a chapter or two?"

Ceretha and Bernadette sat enthralled, while Ruth Ann read. At the end of the third chapter, Ruth put the book down. "Let's call it quits for tonight, girls."

"Miz Logan, I thought my teacher read just about the best in the world, but she cain't hold a candle to you." Bernadette's mother tapped on the kitchen window as she went by. Ruth Ann promised not to read *Alice* again until Bernadette could be present. When Ruth went into the kitchen, Ceretha dialed the number Stuffy had given her. Once the phone started ringing she was tempted to hang up. She thought, I could just as easily write Mrs. Neil a note. Torn between hanging up and hanging on, Ceretha's heart beat just a little faster. There was a click, and someone on the other end said, "Neil-Smith residence."

Ceretha timidly asked, "Is Mrs. Neil in?"

"Who's calling, please?"

Ceretha's first impulse was to say "None of your business," and hang up. She was peeved with herself for having made the call in the first place. Instead of hanging up, however, she gave her name. There was no sound for a second, and then Barbara spoke again. The businesslike quality had gone out of her voice, hesitantly she said, "Ceretha? Oh! Stuffy said you weren't in the hospital any longer. I hope your leg doesn't hurt. I'll call my grandmother to the phone right away."

Barbara put the receiver down before Ceretha even had time to say "thank you." Mrs. Neil was pleased that Ceretha called, and Mama was both surprised and pleased.

In more ways than one, the rest of the week was tiring. Even the new album of Christmas carols which Papa bought, cards from classmates and Sunday school friends, and the making of doll clothes did not make up for having to miss the Harvest Festival at Wickham House. By Thursday, Mama, too, was beginning to show signs of weariness. She and Ceretha went to Dr. Holmes's office. He removed the dressing, and said that he wanted Ceretha to begin walking a bit. "No school until Monday, though. Come back to the office for a final check on Saturday."

Instead of being pleased, as Mama thought she ought to be, Ceretha was moody. To help while the afternoon away, Mama asked about a game of Scrabble. Ceretha submitted, for lack of anything better to do. In spite of herself, she found she was enjoying the game. They were interrupted by a knock on the door. Mama answered with, "Do come in Miss Brailowsky."

"Oh, Nat," Ceretha exclaimed, "I'm so glad you came. Mama, Nat's the first real company we've had since we've been here."

Mama got Nat and Ceretha settled in the living room, and asked, "Won't you have lunch with us, Miss Brailowsky. I'm sorry Papa's not up. He's been wanting to meet you."

Nat was about to refuse when she remembered Ceretha's remark about the first company. "That would be a real treat, but please don't go to a lot of trouble." Nat told Ceretha all about the Harvest Festival, and how Nancy Green had done the "Dying Eagle" solo, but had not done nearly as well as Ceretha.

During lunch, Ceretha hardly got a word in edgewise. Mama wanted to know all about Nat and her family. "Are you Russian?" she asked.

"Yes and no. My father's family originally came from Russia, but they have lived in Poland for several generations now. I was born in Poland. My parents came to America when I was a wee baby."

"Do your parents live here in town?" Mama wanted to know.

"No, Mrs. Brown. They live in a small town in Pennsylvania. I came here to study at the university, and I work at the settlement house—part-time—to help pay my expenses. I am the oldest of eight children, so you see I have to help myself."

"Are you majoring in dancing?"

"Oh, no! Dancing is an avocation for me. My major is social work, but I take all the dance courses I can squeeze in. I was fortunate enough to get into the university's group. I have no illusions about being a really great dancer. I have a younger sister who shows great promise, though. Have you ever thought of Ceretha becoming a dancer? She has a lot of talent."

"Oh, goodness, no," Mama exclaimed. "I don't think her Papa'd like that."

"I haven't really made up my mind what I'd like to be," Ceretha interjected. "I read a book once, *Dancing Shoes*, and it made dancing sound like an exciting career, but a lot of hard work."

"And that it is," Nat agreed. "Would you like to see some pictures of my family? I have my wallet just stuffed with them."

While they were looking at the pictures, Papa joined them. He hadn't said a half dozen words, before he invited Nat to worship with them at their church some Sunday. Nat promised that she would, and shortly thereafter she left, but not before Mama and Papa extracted a promise that she would come back for a real meal one evening. Mama and Ceretha had to repeat for Papa all the things that Nat had said about herself and her family. Papa declared that he could see traits of good and evil reflected in people's faces. "That's a fine young woman; it shows in her face."

Ceretha had not learned, as yet, to be so discerning. She only knew that there were people for whom she felt a real kinship immediately and that Nat was one of these.

14

Ceretha sang in her bath the morning of her return to school. Dr. Holmes was obviously pleased with her progress. There were practically no restrictions, "Just get back into the swing of things gradually," he had said. He saw no reason why she could not run, jump, skip, or dance as long as she did not overdo it at the beginning. Added to this good news was the fact that Ceretha had a new winter coat. She and Bernadette left a little early, so that if Julia was in one of her pokey moods, they'd have time to wait for her. As they emerged from the gangway, they nearly collided with Marlene and Barbara.

Barbara managed a weak, "Hi!" Ceretha declared that Marlene had spoken, too. "Eff she did," Bernadette said, "I didn't hear her." The four of them walked together, and yet apart, as far as Julia's house.

"I like Julia," Barbara said as she and Marlene went on by. "Isn't she in your class?"

"Yes, she's okay. We don't run around together, obviously."

"Obviously," Barbara repeated. "Did you notice Ceretha's coat? I'm getting a new school coat for Christmas. We looked at one just like hers."

"Well for goodness sake don't get one like it!"

"It's a pretty coat, Marlene."

"Okay, it's a pretty coat, but do you want to look like Ceretha?"

"If I have a coat like hers, I still won't look like her."

"True, but speaking of looking like other people. You remember that Mrs. Logan who goes to our church, and works in the law office across from the one where Mother works? That's Ceretha's sister. Would you believe it?"

"Really!"

"The Logans want to buy the Watsons' house. And you know who the Watsons are?"

"Oh, Marlene everybody knows that Attorney Watson is the first Negro City Attorney and that your mother is his secretary. So what?"

Marlene chose to ignore Barbara's lack of enthusiasm. "The Watsons are building a hundred and twenty-five thousand dollar ranch house in Brandonville. They'll be the only Negroes out there."

"How does Yvonne like that?"

"Dope that she is, all she talks about is how far away she'll be from her friends. Now Carla's looking forward to it."

"She would. Carla and me, we don't get along very well."

"I wouldn't exactly call that smart of you. I guess you'd prefer someone like that Ceretha Brown to Carla."

"At least Ceretha's got some brains. All Carla's got is blond hair, gray eyes, and her father's reputation."

"Kitty, kitty," Marlene said, "you're jealous."

Now it was Barbara who chose to do the ignoring. They had reached the school grounds.

Ceretha, Julia, and Bernadette found ever so many things to laugh about that morning as they walked to school. They were not far behind Barbara and Marlene, and were joined by Althea just off the campus. "Kid," she said, "if you hadn't of come to school today, I was going to get your address from Mrs. Hudson. I know you live on Mount Vernon, but I didn't know the number."

"You should have asked Bernadette or Julia."

"Guess I could of, if I'd seen 'em. Don't you hate being sick? I had my tonsils out once, when I was four. My Mom swears I never stopped talking. 'Course I don't remember, four's kind of young. Say, you didn't miss nothing much."

"How do you stand her, Ceretha?" Julia asked jokingly.

"She don't. Guess she's kinda like my Mom, she tolerates me. Don't bother me none."

The four of them had a good belly laugh over this. "Girl," went on Althea, "Miss Goodwin's room looks like a woods or something. She's got autumn leaves, pumpkins, wild flowers—dead and living—gourds . . . you name it, she's got it. The woman's gone autumn-motif crazy. We do 'em with charcoal or watercolor. At first it was fun. We're going to start some dances for the Christmas program."

"According to Marcus, I missed a lot of arithmetic. I just hope Bert can help me catch up."

"Where you see Marcus? That egghead?"

"I didn't see him. He called up one evening."

"Well, now, who'd a thought it? It figures, though, one egghead callin' another one. But you're a kinda nice egghead, but deliver me from Marcus."

In the gym class that afternoon, Ceretha wanted to tell Althea that she was right about her being

167

"tolerated." All day long Althea had usurped the conversation when other children tried to talk to Ceretha about her absence. Ceretha welcomed Miss Parks's whistle which called the class together.

Miss Parks permitted a limited amount of freedom. Ceretha poked Althea with her elbow and nodded her head in Miss Parks's direction.

"Squad leaders, please get your groups quiet. When you have checked the roll and returned it to the office, have your squads sit on the floor."

Althea and Marlene were squad leaders. Marlene had chosen her teammates carefully, so she had a smooth-working group. Althea's squad was made up of the people she liked, regardless of whether or not they'd be able to make any real contribution to the team.

Miss Parks explained that the school was going all out for a Christmas program. The gym classes were furnishing all the dances. The story was built around a well-worn theme: A Night in Santa's Toyshop. There were to be dolls of every nation and a Christmas fairy who was to bring them to life.

"Now," Miss Parks explained, "you and I know that we can't use everybody. We'll use only the best."

Althea stuck her thumbs under her armpits, knowingly. Miss Parks announced tryouts for the part of the fairy queen, to be held after school in two weeks. Ceretha's heart skipped a beat or two.

All the girls who studied ballet were planning to tryout for the part. "I don't stand a ghost of a chance," Ceretha whispered to the girl next to her. And even though she was not talking to her, Althea demanded to know, "Chance at what?"

In the shower room, Ceretha had a chance to explain to Althea that she intended to tryout for the part of the fairy queen. "Honey," Althea stated flatly, "Give it up. You ain't got a chance. First place, you ain't light in color, and you don't have long hair."

"I don't see what color and hair have to do with whether I can dance," Ceretha answered in a huffy tone.

"Don't go hoity-toity on me, kid," Althea came back. "Maybe it didn't make no difference where you came from but you just mark my word. Anyway, you get m' point. If somebody like Carla Watson or Veda Richmond don't get that part, I'll eat my hat."

"Word of honor?" Ceretha asked.

"Girl Scout honor. That's m' best."

Ceretha realized that she and Althea had been joined by someone else. She looked up from fastening her shoe into Marlene's face. Without a word of greeting, Marlene asked, "Are you Mrs. Logan's half sister? We were talking about you over there." She indicated the lockers where Barbara and several others were grouped. "Babs says she's your whole sister. I say she's not."

"Not that it's your business," Ceretha replied, "but she happens to be my whole sister and my only sister." She walked away and left Marlene standing there all red in the face. Althea caught up with Ceretha as quickly as possible. "She's got her nerve. Your sister's married?"

"Where'd you think I got a brother-in-law?"

"Don't get mad with me, kid. Marlene's nuts. Negroes is all kinds of colors. Look at us five Bonds. From jet black to dirty yalla, m' Mom says. We've all got them Bond mouths, though. You can tell one soon as you see 'em."

Ceretha couldn't get home fast enough to tell Mama about Marlene. Julia and Bernadette had offered little or no encouragement when she told them about trying out.

"Well, Ceretha," Julia mused, "go ahead if you want to, but if it turns out like it usually does, Althea won't have to eat her hat. I'll be glad to be in one of the folk dances. I'm pretty sure I'll get chosen for that. You will, too, girl. Why not be satisfied?"

Mama asked, "What are you going to do, Ceretha?"

"Tryout, of course." There was not a second's hesitation between the question and the answer. Ceretha went on to tell Mama about Marlene.

"No use being offended, dear. You're a mixture of my coloring and Papa's, though you look a great deal more like me. Now we may not be as handsome as Papa or as pretty as Ruth Ann, but we hold our own, don't you think? Look at it this way, while it may not have been pleasant, Marlene did talk to you."

"If that's all she can find to talk about, I'd just as soon she didn't talk. But the day wasn't all bad. Aside from the tryouts, we're doing something interesting in art. Is the open-air market still open?"

"It was last weekend, though they don't have much produce. It's getting late in season. Why do you ask?"

"I'd like to get some of those miniature gourds and some other stuff for a Thanksgiving centerpiece."

"Sounds interesting. We're having Thanksgiving dinner at Ruth Ann's, unless Papa rebels. I doubt that he will."

Papa had only one concern. "You roast the bird, Rosie. Not that Ruth Ann can't cook, mind you, I just prefer your turkey to any I've ever eaten." Papa got his way.

That was a Thanksgiving Day to be remembered. Ceretha went with Bertram and Ruth Ann to the services at the Episcopal church. Papa, at first, insisted that Ceretha go with him and Mama. Ruth Ann argued that she never got a chance to

171

take Ceretha to church, since she always went to Sunday school, and when it was over, it was too late to go to St. Mark's. Papa gave in after some gentle persuasion from Mama. Ceretha found the service interesting and a little bit tiring. "I'd never get used to getting up and down so much," she told Ruth and Bert.

In the congregation that morning, were several children she knew from school or from Wickham House. Marlene and her parents sat directly in front of them. After church, Ruth Ann introduced Ceretha to just about everybody in the whole church, Ceretha declared.

When they finally got to the jalopy, Ceretha was full of questions about the service and the difference between the Episcopal church and the Roman Catholic church. "You know something, Miss Rabbit," Bert said in a playful manner, "Papa'd probably explain it better than Ruth or I can. That man never ceases to amaze me with the vast amount of knowledge he's gotten from books. Ask him about it."

"Bert's right, Ceretha," Ruth added, "Papa's got a lot on the ball. By the way, I thought Father Callis' sermon was good."

"Yeah," Bert said. "Generally, he's not much of a preacher. I thought maybe I was impressed because we've got so doggone much to be thankful for today."

Ceretha waited a moment for Bert to elaborate. When she had allowed what she considered to be sufficient time she asked, in a half-whisper, "A baby?"

Ruth Ann's face grew very red. Bert laughed. "Shades of Papa Brown. No, honey, you won't be an auntie for some time to come. We'll tell you all about our big news right after dinner."

"I'm going to have a hard time waiting until then. Can't you just tell me. I promise I won't tell Mama and Papa, please Bert."

Bertram was firm about waiting until after dinner.

"I have some work outlined for you and Bert. I think Mama ought to have an occasional day off, and I'm going to need help."

Bert's first job was to pull out the expanding table in the living room and add the leaves. Ceretha had to inspect the silver, because Ruth did not trust Bert to do a thorough job. She cautioned Bert about the handling of her glassware and china.

"You know what, lil' sis," Bert scoffed, "I suspect that if we weren't having important people like Papa and Mama to dinner, you and I'd be consigned to the kitchen. And what's more, we'd have plain old everyday dishes and stainless steel."

Ruth Ann vowed she'd make them do just that, anyway, if they didn't stop playing. She wanted to sit down to dinner at two. Mama had been up at the crack of dawn to get the big turkey in the oven. Bert and Ceretha had the table finished, with Ceretha's centerpiece, when Mama and Papa came upstairs. Papa was puffing under the weight of the turkey. Once he had got his breath back, Papa had to admire Ceretha's creation for the table. It was made up of a tiny pumpkin, some brightly colored gourds, purple grapes, and some autumn leaves.

The tantalizing smells of the food make it difficult for Ceretha to concentrate, while Papa offered a longer than usual prayer of thanksgiving. Once Ceretha dared to open her eyes and look at Bert, who winked at her. She was in misery for a second or two because she didn't dare snicker. When Papa did end his prayer, they all ate until they could hardly move.

Mama and Papa watched a special on TV while the younger people did the dishes. Papa said he'd like to help, but he'd always been kind of clumsy in the kitchen, and he might just get in the way. Ruth Ann's kitchen was in apple-pie order when she announced that they could now tell their big secret.

Bert made a big thing of clearing his throat. "Oh, go ahead, dear," said Ruth Ann, "you've been looking like the cat that swallowed the canary all day."

Bert liked making a production out of things.

He asked permission to turn off the television, because he needed everybody's undivided attention. Papa's pipe came out of his mouth. Mama sat up erect in her easy chair. Ceretha leaned forward, from her cross-legged position on the floor. Bert at last was ready to speak.

"Mama, Papa, and lil' sister, Ruth and I've got good news."

Papa started to say something. Mama reached over and touched him on the knee. Ceretha snuggled closer to Papa. Bert went on, "We bought a house. Completed the deal yesterday. Three bedrooms, living room, dining room, kitchen, and a bath and a half."

Ruth and Bert couldn't have been any happier about it than Mama and Papa. Both of them had loads of questions to ask.

"What size lot is it on?" Papa wanted to know.

"A big corner lot with large yards, back and front," Ruth Ann answered.

"You're going to like it, Pop. It's a fairly new house. The Watsons have just outgrown it. Why don't we all pile in the jalopy and drive over there? Of course, we won't go inside."

They were putting on their coats when Papa commented, "There's one thing that's bothering me, Bert."

"Yes, Papa?"

"How come that in this proverbial land of the

free, you and Ruth gotta buy in an all colored neighborhood?"

"We combed integrated neighborhoods, Papa. Man, they've upped the prices on those places! This is a nice neighborhood and most of the families are going to stay. They, too, can't swing big mortgage notes right now. I've got to get my degree. I've got my eye on a job in personnel. Things are opening up."

Ruth Ann explained that the Watsons expected to be in their new house before Christmas. "That means we can start our packing right away, so we will be ready to move in just as soon as they move out."

Papa spoke up from the back seat, "Ruth Ann, you and Bert are not expecting your Mama and me to move in with you?"

"That's the general idea," Bert answered. "The house is big enough for all of us."

"Now, Bert," Mama warned, "you and Ruth Ann are wonderful children, and we know you are sincere, but we'll make out where we are until Papa makes a permanent home for us."

Everyone began talking at once. Several times Ruth had to remind Bert to tend to his driving. Ceretha, sandwiched in between Ruth and Bert, felt like weeping.

15

The first snow of the year and the prospect of two Christmas trees to help decorate brightened Ceretha's spirits. She told Bernadette and Julia about Ruth and Bert's new home. They agreed that "grown-up logic" sometimes just didn't make good sense. Julia further consoled Ceretha with, "Anyway, girl, you'd be lonesome over on Whitman Place without Bernadette and me."

They locked arms and trampled down the snow on a walk where it had not been cleared away. Ceretha had actually never seen snow before. In New Hope, the winters were cold and rainy. Some

of the older people there could recall a winter when there had been enough snow to cover the ground, but by noon of the same day it was gone.

"Isn't it beautiful?" Ceretha said gleefully.

"Not going to las' long!" Bernadette added pessimistically.

"Why not? I wish it would stay this way forever and ever—that is, almost forever. If it would only stay white and shiny until we'd wake up one morning and it would be spring."

"Not the way my father grumbles about the oil bill," Julia put in.

"Won't even be white when we come from school," was Bernadette's contribution. "The dirt from the mill, soot from the chimbleys, and people trampin' in it like we're doing, it'll be a mess by lunchtime."

"I hope there's enough left so that we can make

a snowman. I've never made one before," Ceretha said.

"Hey!" Julia shouted. "Isn't this the day of the tryouts?"

"Good gravy, no! You'll scare me half out of my wits. That's next week. Nat's helping me with my dance. That reminds me, Bernadette, did you get chosen for the angel choir?"

"Miss Steward, she didn't tell us yet, but I noticed that she'd stand by some of our desks a longer time, then she'd go to her desk and write something down. She did that by my seat."

"Julia, have you ever heard Bernadette sing?"

"A privilege I've missed. This program's some big deal. My mother's even got her church circle making robes for the choir."

"Mama's going to help with the folk-dance costumes," Ceretha volunteered. "I still can't believe the contest for the fairy queen won't be judged fairly."

At this point, they were joined by Althea and several other children. Althea reminded Ceretha again that fairies in the storybooks always had long golden hair. Ceretha vowed that she didn't care what her friends thought about the idea, she was still going to try for the part. The rules of the contest had been spelled out. Three semifinalists from each of the combined fourth, fifth, and sixth gym classes were to be chosen on Friday. Miss

179

Parks had emphasized over and over again that any girl who wanted to could try out. On the following Monday, the finalists were to perform for five teachers who would act as the judges. The music was from *Swan Lake*, a solo part for the Swan Queen.

Miss Parks felt that she did not want the sole responsibility for choosing the semifinalists, so she had asked the assistant principal to help her.

She had a pretty good idea as to which of the girls would show up for the tryouts. In Ceretha's class she expected Marlene, Celestine, Carla, Yvonne, Marguerite, and one or two others. Barbara Smith took ballet, but was probably too shy to perform before a large audience.

Miss Parks had sized up the situation quite accurately. All of the girls she had named did try out. When all who had volunteered finished, she asked in a tone that implied that she was not expecting an answer, "Is there anyone else who'd like to try out?"

Nat had said, "Shut everything else out, Ceretha. You are the Swan Queen, beautiful, graceful —everything that a dancer needs and wants to be."

Ceretha rose from the floor as if she was in another world. "I'd like to try, Miss Parks," she said, almost inaudibly. It seemed that an age went by in the interim between the time Ceretha danced and Miss Parks called for attention.

Althea commented, "That kid ain't bad!"

Celestine, Yvonne, and Ceretha were chosen to represent their class in the final contest. Ceretha literally danced on air the rest of the day. She couldn't keep her mind on her work. Music from the ballet kept filling her head when she should have been doing something else.

Miss Goodwin scolded, "Ceretha, you've been woolgathering. I asked for designs for Christmas cards. The period's nearly over, and you have absolutely nothing on your paper." There was still nothing on it when the bell rang. At the lockers, Althea cynically cracked, "Give 'em a run for their money, kid, but like I said, don't count on winning."

Julia had already heard the news and was happy. Bernadette had some happiness of her own to share. "I didn't get no solo, but I'm singing a real high part with two other girls in 'Angels We Have Heard on High,' and my name's going to be on the program. How many folks you got to beat to win, Ceretha?"

Ceretha explained that there were nine finalists. The sheer joy of being one of them was almost more than she could bear. While Mama did not share Ceretha's friends' pessimistic view, she did remind her, "You haven't taken ballet lessons and these other girls have. Their training certainly ought to show up."

"But, Mama, there were other girls today who

have taken ballet and I won over them."

"Yes, Brown Rabbit," Mama insisted, while squeezing Ceretha tightly, "I know and I'm proud. Papa, Ruth Ann, and Bert will be proud, but if you don't win, you will have had the thrill of competing."

"But, I've got to win. May I go over to Wickham House and see if Nat can give me a little extra time?"

As luck would have it, Nat was not going to be free until after seven o'clock that evening. She was the only person who shared Ceretha's confidence in her ability to win. On her way home, Ceretha walked right past Stuffy without even seeing him.

"Hey!" he shouted, "What's the matter? It's me. Stuff."

"I'm sorry, Stuff. I'm on cloud nine."

"Yeah! I heard you scored one today. I hope you beat 'em all, especially Marlene. Now there's a girl I really don't like!"

"She was eliminated today, Stuff. She's not even in the running."

"How 'bout that?" He gave Ceretha a sound whack on the back, such as he would have given David, his "jug buddy" if he had been congratulating him. "Hope you beat 'em all, Ceretha. And I better get on to the store or my gram's going to be hoppin' mad."

Ceretha walked on, calculating the hours until

the final contest. Mama went back to Wickham House with her after supper. By that time Nat had told the whole evening staff about her protégé. They worked for an hour. Nat said she didn't want to make too many suggestions, because she wanted Ceretha to dance as she felt it. She walked to the door with Ceretha and Mama. "This little gal's got a lot of talent, Mrs. Brown. Any chance of Mr. Brown being persuaded to let her consider dancing as a profession?"

"I don't think her Papa would ever say she couldn't do it if that was what she chose, but I doubt that he'd be very happy about the choice," Mama answered.

Nobody had to awaken Ceretha on the morning of the contest. She kept Papa and Mama in stitches at the breakfast table telling about how she had spent the night dreaming of being an ugly duckling who was turned into a beautiful swan by a handsome prince. Mama said the elaboration of the dream was to cover up for the little bit of breakfast Ceretha was eating. Bernadette was as excited as Ceretha. Ruth Ann stopped in to wish her sister luck and to tell her that she had sent for tickets to the *Nutcracker* for the day after Christmas. "I sent for six tickets, Bernadette," Ruth Ann said, "I should have asked your mother first, but I hope she'll let you go." Bernadette was positive that she'd be able to go, "Just to make sure, Miz Logan, I'll be extry, special good from now until Christmas."

Most mornings Ceretha, Bernadette, Barbara, and Marlene were within a few feet of each other, at least as far as Julia's house. This morning Ceretha sensed that her name came up frequently.

Julia was waiting on her steps for them. She, too, was caught up in the excitement of the day. Bernadette and Julia did most of the talking. They offered every word of encouragement they could think of until Ceretha pleaded with them to find another subject. "Feel my heart," she said, "I don't believe I'll make it until three o'clock."

On a rail in front of the school, in spite of the snow, sat Marlene, Barbara, Celestine, Yvonne, and Carla.. Celestine got up when she saw Ceretha and her friends. In her sweetest, most polite tone, she asked, "Ceretha, may I talk to you alone."

Bernadette and Julia saw no need for it. Ceretha was in a quandary, for a moment, "Wait for me!" Celestine gulped, once or twice. "The other night at dinner I told my mother and father about your dancing."

"Oh!"

"My father thought he might have met your father at a NAACP meeting."

"Maybe."

"What I'm trying to tell you, Ceretha, is that I told my parents how mean we had been to you."

"Your were n—"

"Let me finish, please." Celestine was on the verge of tears. "My mother said there was only one way to right a wrong and that was to take the bull by the horns and admit that you made a mistake. I've been trying to do that ever since that night."

"What I started to say, Celestine, was that you were never really nasty to me."

"I wasn't nice, either, and my Mom and Dad said that was just as great a crime. I'd like to make it up to you, if I can."

Ceretha offered Celestine her hand, which Celestine took. The two turned back toward the rest of the group. "There's one other thing," Celestine said, "our Scout Troop is going caroling the Tuesday after school is out. Mrs. Kigh has said that we may invite guests, as long as we don't ask troublemakers. I'd like for you and Julia to come."

"And Bernadette, too?" Ceretha asked.

"And Bernadette, too!" Celestine repeated. "I feel a hundred pounds lighter. Should I tell Julia and Bernadette, or will you?"

"Why don't you?"

Ceretha survived the day without the threatened "heart attack." Only the contestants were admitted to the auditorium that afternoon. Celestine and Yvonne were just ahead of Ceretha as they walked in. "Come on, Ceretha," Celestine called, "Are you as scared as we are?"

Ceretha knew that she had to be more fright-

ened than anybody in that room. The five judges were scattered about the room. Miss Parks had the girls draw lots for their turns to dance. Ceretha drew number eight. Just to prolong the agony, she thought. Joan Rodgers, a fourth grader, was number one. Ceretha would like to have traded with her. Joan seemed very sure of herself, and Ceretha thought her dance was very good. Yvonne, the only girl on-toe, was number five. Ceretha had gone into "outer space" between Joan's number and Yvonne's. Her hands were wringing wet and her mouth was dry. "Oh, golly," she thought, "six, seven, eight."

Yvonne's toe-shoes hampered rather than helped her dance. Ceretha thought she had done much better in the gym. "Number eight, number eight," Miss Parks said twice before Ceretha realized that she was being called. Her confidence was gone; every step toward the stage was torture. "You're the Swan Queen, breathe deeply, the butterflies will go, walk with grace and beauty." These things were all things that Nat had said. The music began once more for the eighth time.

Ceretha remembered only the beginning and the end. When she was back in her seat, Yvonne touched her and whispered, "I hate to admit it, but I think you've got it." The ninth girl had danced, and Miss Parks collected the judges' tallies. "Girls," she said finally, "You've been patient. And every

187

one of you was good. We wish that we could use all nine of you. But the script calls for one fairy. Perhaps, at another time, we will be able to use all of our ballerinas. This time the unanimous decision of the judges is for number eight, Ceretha Brown, with Joan Rodgers as runner-up and alternate. Mrs. Prescott would like to see Ceretha and Joan for a moment. The rest of you are excused."

Mrs. Prescott gave Ceretha and Joan scripts and the rehearsal schedule. They walked from the auditorium, hand in hand, talking quietly. Outside in the snow, waiting for each, was a small group of friends. Hurrying toward Ceretha were Celestine, Julia and Bernadette.

Evangeline Morse

When Evangeline Morse was four years old, her family moved from Georgia to Chicago, Illinois. Her father, a Congregational minister, used to say that as soon as she learned to talk she asked for a pencil. There may be something in his story, for Miss Morse has been writing or drawing for as long as she can remember. She wrote most of the plays produced by the young people's group at the Lincoln Memorial Church while in her teens.

Miss Morse graduated from high school during the Depression, and her parents urged her to choose a career which would give her some measure of security rather than go into the creative arts. She is a graduate of Talladega College and the Chicago Theological Seminary.

Her interest and concern for children eventually led her into social work. She worked in a settlement house for some years, before she joined the staff of the Gary, Indiana, public schools as a social worker.